W9-CEP-057

A TIME TO FIGHT BACK

True Stories of Wartime Resistance

A TIME TO FIGHT BACK

True Stories of Wartime Resistance

JAYNE PETTIT

Houghton Mifflin Company
Boston 1996

For information about this and other Houghton Mifflin
trade and reference books and multimedia products, visit
The Bookstore at Houghton Mifflin on the World Wide
Web at http://www.hmco.com/trade/.

Manufactured in the United States of America
Book design by Celia Chetham
The text of this book is set in 11.75 pt. Galliard
BP   10   9   8   7   6   5   4   3   2   1

Library of Congress Cataloging-in-Publication Data
Pettit, Jayne.
A time to fight back: true stories of wartime resistance /
Jayne Pettit.
p.   cm.
ISBN 0-395-76504-8 (hardcover)
1. World War, 1939–1945 — Children—Juvenile literature.
2. World War, 1939–1945 — Underground movements —
Juvenile literature.   3. World War, 1939–1945 — Personal
narratives — Juvenile literature.   4. World War, 1939–1945 —
Prisoners and prisons — Juvenile literature.   I. Title.
D810.C4P47   1996
940.53'161 — dc20   95-34381   CIP   AC

To my grandchildren,
Julianne, Jeremy and Geoffrey,
Alyssa, Alexandra and Tess

Acknowledgments

The author is deeply grateful to Mary Hardy, research librarian at the Howe Library in Hanover, New Hampshire, for her generous assistance over the period of many months of investigation and to all of those at the Baker Library at Dartmouth College. Special thanks to Barrie Van Dyck for her valuable suggestions, Mandy Little who brought my work to the attention of Macmillan's Children's Books, and to Matilda Welter, my editor at Houghton Mifflin Company, for her wise and encouraging commentary. And finally, a word of appreciation to my husband, Bin, for his patience, understanding and support.

Contents

Introduction

During the late 1920s, an embittered little Austrian by
the name of Adolf Hitler set the stage for a nightmare
that would one day reach to the far corners of the
globe. To the crowds that gathered in towns and cities
throughout Germany, Hitler spoke of his dream — a
Third Reich, or empire, as he called it, that would last
for a thousand years.

Year by year, Hitler's influence continued to grow.
By 1930, he and his followers in the National Socialist
German Workers' Party (the Nazis) had won important seats in the government. By 1933, Adolf Hitler
had seized complete control of the leadership.

In the months that followed, thousands of people
who opposed the Nazi regime were arrested and
many were executed. Books were burned, newspapers
and radio stations were nationalized, and teachers

throughout the country were ordered to teach the Nazi propaganda.

As Hitler and the Nazis increased their power over the people, the Jews of Germany were among the first to be persecuted, because they were considered to be an inferior race. Lawyers and physicians lost their practices; university professors were denied their positions. Forced to wear the Star of David on their clothing, Jews were no longer permitted to use public transportation and their children were barred from attending school.

In 1938, Hitler and his armies marched into Austria. By the following year, Czechoslovakia and Poland had fallen to the Nazis, and in 1940, Denmark, Norway, the Netherlands and Belgium were overtaken. World War II had begun in earnest. As the Nazi terror swept through country after country, Jews everywhere were cut off from the rest of society. Eventually, millions of them would die in the gas chambers, along with gypsies, the handicapped, and anyone else the Nazis considered to be inferior.

Between 1939 and 1945, countless numbers of children suffered the hardships and the horrors of World War II. In England, more than a million children were separated from their families when they were evacuated from London and other major cities under bombardment from German air raids during the Blitz. Many of those who stayed behind were orphaned or killed.

Children in the occupied countries of Europe learned the pain of hunger and disease as the Germans confiscated food supplies, livestock, and fuel to supply their armies. Millions of children in Belgium, France, the Netherlands, Czechoslovakia, and Poland were sent into slave labor in German factories. As war spread throughout Asia and the South Pacific, untold numbers of children lost their lives.

In the midst of this seemingly endless night, there were children throughout Europe and elsewhere who waged their own battles against the forces of evil. Young people risked their lives to carry secret messages back and forth between units working in the Resistance. Others smuggled food to people in hiding and still others helped to blow up bridges, ammunitions factories, and railway lines. In Nazi-occupied Denmark, a group of brave young boys printed an underground newspaper, sabotaged enemy barracks, stole weapons, and even set fire to a train carrying German military supplies!

A Time to Fight Back focuses on the experiences of

eight children caught in the web of World War II. In France, a deaf mute rescued a downed American fighter pilot. In Belgium, a twelve-year-old boy distributed an underground newspaper carrying secret messages, and in Scotland, a young teenager wrote of her fears of a German invasion on her island. Of the others, one spent the war years in hiding, another was a prisoner at Auschwitz, and still another was a victim of bombing raids over Germany. In our own country, a British boy was one of thousands of children who found a home away from home during the Blitz. And a five-year-old Japanese American endured three and a half years of hardship behind barbed wire in a California detention camp with her family and thousands of others of her race.

Each of the following stories is true. Each is a tale of remarkable courage.

The Secret Messenger

In May of 1940, the little country of Belgium found itself overrun by the German armies for the second time in less than twenty-five years. The people of Belgium, defiant yet powerless in the face of such an overwhelming enemy, lost no time in forming underground organizations in every village, town, and city throughout the land.

During the months that followed, the Germans began mass deportations of the country's 45,000 Jews, but not without strong resistance from Belgian patriots. Men and women in every walk of life came to the rescue of thousands of Jewish men, women and children. The Dowager Queen Elizabeth of Belgium used her influence to save hundreds of Jews. Catholic and Protestant churches found hiding places for Jews in convents, monasteries, and in private homes. Railroad workers derailed deportation trains heading out of the country and police officers provided false identification papers for those who went into hiding. As a result of these efforts, nearly half of the total Jewish population was saved.

Soon after their arrival in Belgium, the Nazis seized control of all newspapers and radio stations in the country, cutting off vital lifelines of communication between the Belgian people. Soon, hundreds of underground printing presses went into operation in cellars and out of the way places everywhere.

In the city of Brussels, now jammed with armed vehicles and tanks and roving units of the German secret police, twelve-year-old Peter Brouet lived with his mother and father on a quiet street not far from a lovely park. For as long as he could remember, Peter had listened to stories of his grandfather's experiences as an editor of a secret newspaper during the First World War.

There were many editors of that paper, Peter's father would tell him, because in spite of the fact that the printing presses were frequently moved in order to avoid discovery, German spies would get word of their whereabouts and destroy the equipment. The editors would then be lined up in the streets and executed. Young Peter Brouet was no stranger to the risks involved in publishing the newspaper. His own grandfather had been one of those editors who had been shot.

The publication and distribution of *La Libre Belgique*, or *Free Belgium*, remained a mystery to all who read it. Housewives returning from the marketplace would find copies of the paper tucked into their shopping baskets. Business people and passengers on trains and trolley cars would discover the paper smuggled into their coat pockets. Homeowners leaving for work each morning would find that someone had slipped *La Libre* through their mail slots during the night. Most amazing was the fact that even after the destruction of the paper's presses and the execution of its editors, *La Libre Belgique* would soon appear in every corner of the city. Somehow, new equipment would go into operation, and new editors would replace those whose lives had been lost.

La Libre Belgique and others like it became a strong link between the people of Belgium for several reasons. In addition to bringing them news from the war front or of events taking place in their country, the newspaper gave out coded information from underground resistance groups, relayed disguised messages between Belgian patriots, and urged citizens to band together in the cause of freedom.

The unknown editor of this remarkable little paper

always signed himself "Peter Pan," after the mischievous boy in the much loved children's story, and from time to time he enjoyed playing a joke on the German oppressors. Once, he suggested to his readers that if ever they had a problem with the secret police they should contact a gentleman by the name of Monsieur Vesalius at the *Place des Barricades.*

The tyrannical commandant of the German Occupational Forces, General Friedrich von Falkenhausen, at once rushed to the *Place des Barricades* with a squad of secret police only to find that Monsieur Vesalius was nothing but a bronze statue!

For years, Peter and his father would act out the story of *La Belgique* and the mysteries surrounding it. Switching roles, each would take turns at being editor, newspaper boy, or even the hated General von Falkenhausen. Each time, they would find new ways to send secret messages or hide their paper in unlikely places around the house.

One day, when Peter was eight years old, he went down to his cellar and set up the toy printing press that his father and mother had given him for Christmas. He had decided to write an article about someone whose name was frequently mentioned in discussions between his parents. In the article, Peter warned the people of Belgium of a man whose armies would one day invade their country if its citizens weren't careful. The man was Adolf Hitler and the year was 1935.

Peter finished his work, and, after signing it "Peter Pan," put the printing press back in its secret hiding place, tiptoed up to his father's study and knocked on the door.

When Peter heard his father's voice inviting him in, he opened the door with great flourish and entered the room. Bowing low and clicking his heels, he addressed his father as "Herr General."

Immediately recognizing the start of a new round of their old game, Monsieur Brouet spun around in his chair and roared at his son. How had this stranger managed to slip past the guards? And what was the reason for his presence?

Just as quickly, Peter greeted the "General" once again, this time adding that he was the "tailor" who had mended the officer's coat pocket the week before.

Continuing the game, Peter's father pretended to ignore him, but not before unbuttoning his coat pocket. With this, the boy tucked his fresh copy of *La Libre Belgique* into the gaping pocket. And as he did so, a strong arm reached out to grab him.

Accusing Peter of being an enemy spy, the "General" pulled the paper from his jacket, read it, and threatened to deliver him to the firing squad.

And then, as the role-playing ended, Peter's father told him yet another tale of General von Falkenhausen and his troubles with *La Libre Belgique*. Each morning, as the paper found its way to the general's desk, he would go into a fit of rage, issuing orders for the immediate arrest of the unknown editor. But despite all of the threats, General von Falkenhausen never did locate the mysterious culprit, nor did he discover who had delivered the paper. After the war, the truth was revealed. As it happened, one of *La Libre*'s couriers was the old scrubwoman who cleaned his office. Hiding the paper in her apron, she would place it on the general's desk when she had finished her chores.

As the years passed, the menace of Hitler and his followers increased. Throughout the countries of Europe, people everywhere sensed the approach of yet another war with Germany. And then, in 1938, the Nazis marched into Austria. In the following year Czechoslovakia was overtaken, and then came the collapse of Poland.

On the morning of May 10, 1940, as the pale light of dawn crept across the skies, Hitler and his mighty armies invaded Belgium, Denmark, The Netherlands and little Luxembourg. In each country, the people put up a brave fight but they were no match against the awesome power of the German military. World War II had begun.

Within weeks, the click of polished boots could be heard in the streets of Brussels as Nazi soldiers in smartly pressed uniforms marched through the city. The people turned out by the thousands, hands clenched and faces taut with hatred.

The highly organized invaders moved in quickly. Loudspeakers blasted out orders to the people, warning them of the swift arrest and immediate execution of those who tried to defy the enemy. Curfews went into effect and notices on public buildings issued rules for the rationing of food. And that was just the beginning.

By a strange twist of fate, the new commandant of the German Occupational forces was none other than the nephew of the dreaded General von Falkenhausen. Immediately, he ordered that any pages describing the invasion of Belgium during the First World War be torn out of the history books used in the schools.

Soon after the arrival of the Germans, the Belgian people felt the grip of hunger as livestock and food supplies left the country by the trainload for delivery to the German armies and their families abroad. Each day, shopkeepers in stores everywhere struggled to find foods for their customers and the lines in front of empty shop windows grew longer and longer.

The scarcity of food soon began to take a heavy toll on Belgium's school children, who often had to go to bed hungry. Many of the students, weakened from the lack of nourishment, fainted in class. For Jewish children, the problem was even greater because the Germans made certain that the amount of food issued to Jewish families was substantially less than that issued to other Belgians.

As matters grew worse, Peter Brouet returned from school one day and told his parents that his best friend, Jules Solomon, had fainted in class that morning. Peter was concerned and upset because Jules would not accept the food that he had offered to share with him.

At dinnertime that evening, Peter's mother went next door to the Solomons' house with a small basket of food. When Mrs. Solomon saw the basket, she was embarrassed and vigorously protested the offering. Finally, when Mrs. Brouet informed her that Jules had become ill in school that day, the distraught mother gave in and accepted the basket.

Not long after the incident, Jules did not come to class one day. When school was dismissed that afternoon, Peter ran home and hopped the wall between his house and the Solomons' to find Jules sitting in the back yard poring over an arithmetic assignment. When Peter asked his friend why he hadn't been in school, the boy told him that General von Falkenhausen had just issued a new order. Jewish students were no longer allowed to attend school.

With that, Peter reached into his school bag and brought out his own book, some paper and two pencils. Minutes later, the two young boys were sitting together in the cellar of the Solomon home solving problems that Peter had learned in class that morning. For the next several days, Peter Brouet rushed home from school each afternoon, pulled his school books from his sack, and went next door to the Solomons' cellar to study in secrecy with his friend.

Then one afternoon, it happened. As neighbors up and down the quiet street watched from behind half closed window blinds, an unmarked car pulled up to the Solomon house. The car stopped, the doors opened, and from it emerged several of General von Falkenhausen's uniformed secret police. Within a short time, the Solomons — Jules, his baby sister, and his parents — were seen walking down the steps and into the police car. The car sped off, and the Solomons were never seen again.

All over Belgium, people were distressed by the events that were taking place. For those who openly defied the German invaders, public executions of hundreds of Belgian patriots took place, and many citizens began to lose hope.

And then, early one morning, men and women throughout the city of Brussels awakened to find their mailboxes jammed with the pages of a newspaper. *La Libre Belgique* was back!

During the months that followed, copies of the paper were distributed to homes and businesses everywhere. Just as in World War I, housewives found them in their market baskets, passengers on trains and trolley cars discovered them in their pockets, and school teachers found them on their desks. This time, however, with improved equipment, the newspaper could be printed more efficiently. And if word reached its editors of an impending raid by the Gestapo, the presses could be quickly dismantled and whisked by car to a new location.

Once again, Peter Brouet's father became involved with the work of the underground newspaper, but in a different way. During World War I, Monsieur Brouet had been one of thousands of schoolchildren who had helped to distribute the paper. Now he was one of the editors.

One day, Monsieur Brouet came home from his stationery shop worried and distressed. When his wife asked him what was troubling him, he replied that some neighborhoods in the city were not getting enough copies of the paper. Madame Brouet, who had become active in smuggling *La Libre* to women in marketplaces all over Brussels, suggested that she could get additional women to help her. Children might also help with the work, Monsieur Brouet added.

As time passed, the number of people involved with the distribution of the secret paper increased. But Peter's father and mother began to notice a change in him. The boy had grown quieter and more serious than in the past and was often away from home for hours at a time. When he did appear, he seemed tired and had little to say.

And then one morning at breakfast, Peter explained the reasons for his mysterious behavior. For weeks, he and a group of friends had been helping to deliver the newspaper!

Madame Brouet and her husband were worried about their son. They knew the risks involved in their work, and that swift reprisals followed the arrest of those who were working in the Belgian underground. It was not uncommon for children to be executed for their part in the movement. But, they argued, if other boys and girls were willing to take those risks, how could they prevent Peter from helping? And besides, Monsieur Brouet went on to explain, he and his son had spent years preparing for times like these. When it came to the smuggling of the newspaper, Peter had learned all the tricks of the trade and had invented a few of his own.

The next night, as the people of Brussels lay sleeping, the sounds of air raid sirens pierced the air. Peter and his parents, awakened by the noise, hurried to their cellar. As they watched through their darkened windows, white trails of searchlights darted through the skies and the blasts of anti-aircraft guns shook the ground.

Then, a short distance away, a lone plane dropped from the sky, its propeller sputtering and its wings in flames. Seconds later, it crashed in a brilliant burst of fire. The next morning the people of Brussels learned what had happened. A British airman returning from a raid over Germany had become separated from his squadron. The pilot, unable to eject from his plane, had been killed.

From all over the city, men, women, and children walked to the scene of the crash. In their arms they carried flowers from their gardens. Reaching the downed aircraft, the people laid the flowers at the site, and stood with bowed heads and hands held in tribute to their fallen ally. Each day the crowds of people increased, and each day the Germans patrolling the area grew angrier. Finally, at the orders of General von Falkenhausen, the plane was hauled away.

The next morning, more people gathered at the crash site, and fresh flowers appeared. General von Falkenhausen, infuriated by the defiance of the Belgians, ordered the immediate arrest of anyone caught at the scene.

The editors of *La Libre Belgique* went into action. A special edition of the underground paper appeared, telling readers to continue their act of defiance. The message to the people of Brussels was simple and direct: *Take to the streetcars!*

At home, Peter and his parents worked for hours, bundling copies for distribution. Then each went in a different direction; Madame Brouet to her marketplace, and Monsieur Brouet to other parts of the city. Peter waited until the evening curfew had sounded and then stole through the darkness with his group, up one street and down another, darting from doorway to doorway to push their papers through each mail slot. At the sound of an approaching vehicle, the group separated, slipping into alleyways in practiced silence.

Peter and the others worked throughout the night to deliver the paper, running back to the house for fresh bundles when their supplies ran low. With the first light of day, they returned to their homes to catch a few brief hours of sleep.

Later that day, the three Brouets left their house and walked to the nearest streetcar terminal, where a large crowd had assembled. Quickly and quietly the people boarded one or another of the five cars waiting in line at the curb. Peter and his parents moved to the fifth car and waited for the column to progress through the city to the site of the downed plane. Then, as each streetcar approached the scene, it slowed to a halt. Soon, other streetcars arrived from all over the city. At a signal, the conductors switched off their engines and the people rose in silence with heads bowed and hands clasped behind them.

German soldiers swarmed around the cars, their rifle butts banging on the windows, but the people refused to budge from their positions. Furious, the soldiers demanded that the locked doors be opened and shouted at the conductors to move on or face arrest.

Minutes passed, and nothing happened. And then, slowly, the streetcar in the front of the column began to creep forward, and then another and another until all of the cars had left the curb. The passengers continued to keep their vigil, standing defiantly by their seats, eyes fixed on the sentries outside.

Once again, *La Libre Belgique* had accomplished its work. Once again, the citizens of the little country of Belgium had acted together in the only way they could to resist a powerful and seemingly indestructible enemy. And Peter Pan Brouet, who had been named in honor of the original editor, had been a part of it all.

The Hidden

The people of Lublin, Poland, could trace their city's history back to medieval times when a cluster of peasants' houses and shops sprang up around the hilltop castle of the fourteenth-century king, Kazimierz the Great. Several hundred years later, Lublin had developed into a thriving metropolis of 200,000.

One section of the city was composed of factories, stores, and craft shops, and there were several neighborhoods where most of the merchants and business people lived. In addition, there was the ghetto area where a large percentage of the Jews of Lublin resided.

Eight-year-old Nechama Bawnik and her older sister lived with their parents in the prosperous and predominantly Christian area of the city. Their apartment house on a side street just off of the main avenue was surrounded by gracious modern buildings, tree-lined parks and shops catering to the wealthy.

Nechama's father was a brilliant man and the owner of two factories. As a student at the university, he had once trained for the rabbinate. A highly respected member of the business community, Roman Bawnik was known for his quiet strength and his devotion to his family.

Nechama's mother was a compassionate and deeply religious woman who clung to the traditions of the past and left the education of her daughters entirely in the hands of her husband.

Little Nechama had learned about anti-Semitism at an early age. More than once she had watched roving gangs of Polish teenagers smashing the windows of Jewish businesses and shouting obscene words at the owners inside. When Nechama discussed these happenings with her father, he would explain that many people in Poland did not like the Jews. He would also tell her that being born a Jew was nothing she should be ashamed of.

Nechama and her sister attended a private school in Lublin along with other students from prominent Jewish families. Unlike her sister, she was not a good student, and much preferred playing in the park while her governess met with other governesses to discuss the events of the day. Sometimes, Nechama overheard the women talk about their fears of another war in Europe.

On Friday and Saturday evenings, Nechama's home was filled with family members and good friends who gathered regularly for discussions around a table abundant with rich pastries and sweets of every kind. On most occasions, the conversation also centered around rumors of war and Hitler's hatred of the Jews. During these discussions, Nechama stayed close to her father, listening uneasily to all that was said.

On September 1, 1939, Hitler invaded Poland, and Nechama's well-protected world came to an abrupt end. Air raid sirens broke through the calm of the late summer afternoon, and just as the Bawnik family raced to the cellar of the apartment house, a bomb exploded nearby, shaking the building and shattering windows.

The bombings continued for days, while the Polish army tried in vain to resist the attack. Within a week, the fighting in Lublin ended, and just as quickly the streets of the city were swarming with German soldiers. On September 17, Russia, at that time Germany's ally, attacked Poland from her eastern border, and by October 5, the country had surrendered to the Germans in the west and the Russians in the east.

An uneasy quiet followed. But the German presence was ominous and the atmosphere was tense. Refugees from the west arrived by the hundreds with tales of

German atrocities and the news circulated of Hitler's
determination to rid Europe of all Jews.

Each day, the Germans tightened their hold on the
Polish people, whom they considered inferior because,
unlike other Europeans, the Polish were members of
the Slavic race. Polish Jews, however, suffered the
greatest hardships.

Within weeks of the takeover, many Jewish businesses, stores, and factories were shut down or placed
under German commissioners. Jewish children were
forbidden to attend school, homes were raided, and
private belongings were confiscated. Nechama's parents discussed the possibility of moving the family to
the Russian sector of the country where conditions
at that time were less threatening. A decision was
reached. Nechama's father would travel to Kovel, a
Russian-occupied city, to investigate matters there.

While Mr. Bawnik was away, Nechama's mother
took charge of a small candle factory that the family
still owned. One morning, Mrs. Bawnik reached the
factory to find its doors locked and posted with German orders forbidding entrance. Knowing that a Jewish employee who had worked the night shift was
trapped inside the building, she hastily unlocked the
door and released the man. Then, just as she started to

replace the lock, a Gestapo agent suddenly appeared and beat her until she fell to the ground. While the attack was taking place, several people in homes nearby witnessed what was happening but knew that any attempt to defend the woman would be useless. Finally, the German left, and two men rushed from their houses, lifted the brutally battered woman into a passing carriage, and took her home.

When Mrs. Bawnik was carried into the apartment, she was almost unrecognizable. Seeing her swollen and bloodied body, Nechama was shocked and terrified at what the Nazi had done to her mother. As she watched the woman lying on her bed, unable to move and barely able to speak, she was filled with anger.

Gradually, Mrs. Bawnik regained her strength, determined to put the beating behind her and instructing her daughters to behave as if nothing had happened. And then, for some unexplained reason, the Germans reopened the little candle factory and Nechama's mother, fully recovered, was once again in charge.

Nechama's father returned from Kovel to tell the family that he had decided not to move them. But when Hans Frank, the German governor-general appointed by Hitler, sealed the border between the

Russian and Polish sectors and began ordering Jews into isolated ghettos, Roman Bawnik realized that he had made a terrible mistake.

Of the two factories owned by Nechama's family, the larger one manufactured chemicals. With the German takeover of Jewish factories that were considered essential to the war effort, a German commissioner was assigned to supervise operations at the chemical factory. Nechama's father refused to work for him and resigned from his duties.

As time went by, however, it became obvious that work was a matter of life and death. Those Jews who had been unable to find new employment were often sent off to German labor camps. Others simply disappeared. Nechama's father soon came to realize that for the safety of his family, he would have to get work at the factory.

When Mr. Bawnik went to see the German commissioner, he was told that he had come too late and that all of the jobs were filled. A long silence followed, and finally, without comment, Mr. Bawnik got up from his chair to leave. But as he reached the office door, the German suddenly changed his mind. A job could be found after all, and the identification papers so necessary for survival would be provided.

With her husband now employed at the factory, Mrs. Bawnik decided that for further protection of her family, she too would look for work that would allow her to carry identification papers. Finding a job as a housekeeper for a high-ranking Nazi officer, she proved herself to be such a fine worker that her employers took to giving her food baskets to supplement the meager provisions she was able to find in the stores.

Conditions in the city of Lublin were becoming desperate. From conversations that she overheard in her employers' house, Nechama's mother learned of increased deportations, executions, and disappearances. Finally, the section of the city in which Nechama and her family lived became forbidden to Jews under an edict called *Judenrein,* or free of Jews. Having nowhere to go, the Bawniks were offered a room that was one of three in an apartment in the Jewish quarter of the city. In time, more people arrived to settle into the other two rooms. A tiny kitchen was shared by the three families.

Nechama's parents, worried that their daughters' education was suffering because they were no longer allowed to attend school, hired a young woman by the name of Hela Trachtenberg. Like other Jewish teachers and university professors, Hela had been dismissed from her position in Warsaw. The girls took to her instantly and the three soon became fast friends.

Each day for four hours Nechama and her sister studied Latin, mathematics, science, and literature. Urged on by Hela's gentle ways and soft-spoken humor, Nechama soon began to take a serious interest in her studies. But there were great risks involved. The Germans, in addition to closing schools to Jewish students, had also banned private instruction in the home. For Nechama and anyone caught in this forbidden activity, the penalty was death by firing squad.

One evening after the Bawnik family had settled into their cramped room in the Jewish sector, Nechama's mother rushed home from work with alarming news. The German officer's wife had told her that she could no longer employ her. Then, in a sobbing voice, the woman had warned her of a raid that would take place late that night.

After a few brief words, Nechama's parents gathered together what few items they could carry, including the heavy coats into which Nechama's mother had sewn money and most of the family jewelry. Minutes later, the Bawniks left the little room that had been their brief refuge and walked silently into the darkness.

Later, at the chemical factory, the German commissioner greeted Nechama and her family kindly and promised that he would protect them. A large, empty room on the second floor would provide a safe hiding place, and in the morning Nechama's mother and sister would be given work in the factory. All would be well, he assured everyone.

As the German turned to leave, Mr. Bawnik pulled from his coat pocket a small cloth bag containing jewelry and gold. Presenting it to the man, Nechama's father asked that it be kept for future use in case of trouble. The official agreed to accept the bag, promising that he would return it if it were needed.

A Polish janitor who lived in the building with his wife brought mattresses for the family to sleep on until he could find a few additional furnishings. Everyone settled down gratefully and tried not to think of what might be happening back in the ghetto.

The next morning, Nechama and the others learned what had occurred. Soon after they had escaped to the factory, German SS troops stormed the ghetto and ordered the entire Jewish population into the streets. Then, as in all raids, families were separated from one another and babies from their mothers. Beatings followed, and those who could no longer stand were

shot. Of those who remained, the wounded were deported to concentration camps and the rest were sent
to a new ghetto, a labor camp called Majdan Tatarski.
Hela Trachtenberg, Nechama's beloved tutor and
friend who had also found a room in Lublin's Jewish
sector, had been sent to the labor camp.

For the next year, the Bawnik family continued to
live in the deserted room at the factory. Nechama's
parents and her sister worked long hours, and the days
were empty and lonely. Outside, the little girl could
hear the sounds of children's voices as they played in a
schoolyard not far from the building. For a time, the
sounds of the students' laughter provided comfort and
served as a reminder of the happy life she had once
led. But soon, the voices began to depress her and
made her fearful of what the future might bring.

The year 1942 was drawing to a close. During the
time that Nechama and her family found shelter at the
factory, one disaster had followed another. Many of
Nechama's relatives throughout Poland had either lost
their lives or had been deported. And during a raid on
the labor camp at Majdan Tatarski, Hela Trachtenberg
had been beaten and shot to death.

As these events unfolded, Nechama's father came to the conclusion that the only way the family could survive would be to go into hiding in Warsaw. There, with the help of a Polish Christian, they might be able to live out the war.

Then one day, a cousin who lived in Warsaw visited the factory and offered the Bawniks space in his apartment there. The cousin, although Jewish, had amassed a small fortune in undercover business dealings with a number of German officers. Because of his connections, the cousin told Nechama's father that he could provide them with a safe hiding place.

After two days of discussions, the plans to go into hiding in Warsaw were finalized. A short time later, carrying false identification papers and new names that described them as Christian Poles, Nechama and her family were on their way.

Nechama's cousin Bolek, a big, cheerful man with a ready smile and exuberant ways, lived in an expensively furnished apartment on one of Warsaw's finest streets. Nechama and her family were given a room in which to live and a kitchen that they were to share with several other people who had moved in.

After days of watching families come and go,

Nechama and her family learned that Bolek's apartment had become a processing center for Jews searching for a hiding place. Bolek supplied food and false papers to all who needed them and a bed on which to sleep until living arrangements could be made. As an extra precaution, Bolek gave Nechama and her family new papers as well as new names.

For the next several days, the rules for survival had to be learned. Names, birthdates and birthplaces were memorized, and under no circumstances could actual names be used. Family background, relatives, and occupation were fabricated for protection in the event of an interrogation.

Because they were "passing" as Christian Poles, Nechama and her family had to memorize the prayers, doctrines, and rituals of the Catholic church, to which the majority of the Polish people belonged. This took time but was an essential part of the process. It was well known that many Jews had lost their lives because they had failed to learn these facts. Everyone practiced in earnest and tested one another repeatedly. The slightest mistake or hesitation would mean death or deportation.

In time, Nechama's father, ever cautious and on the alert, grew anxious about the living situation in Bolek's apartment. With so many people moving in and out, one slip-up could bring disaster. If someone in the apartment were arrested, the names of all of the others staying there might be revealed. Nechama's father was also concerned about Bolek's dealings with the Germans and with the fact that Warsaw had become a center for Jews going into hiding.

Bolek, as understanding as always, set about to find a house outside of the city. After a considerable search, he found a couple who would take the risk of hiding the family for an exorbitant sum. Nechama's parents agreed to pay the price of protection.

Jan and Magda lived in a tiny, two-room apartment just outside of Warsaw. There were two advantages to the situation. The couple had no children and no one ever visited.

The Bawniks moved into one of the two rooms and tried to settle themselves. Nechama's father, whose blond hair and blue eyes belied his Jewish heritage, was the only member of the family who could venture out of the apartment. Through contacts he had made with people in Warsaw, he was able to keep in touch with events as they were occurring.

Returning to the apartment one evening, Mr. Bawnik told of the death of his friend and former business partner back in Lublin. The partner, along with his daughter and son-in-law, had been in hiding in Warsaw. Later on, the daughter and her husband would also be killed.

The strain of living with Jan and Magda slowly began to affect everyone. Jan, an unemployed laborer with a violent temper, constantly fought with his wife. There were frequent beatings, and Magda's face was often swollen with bruises.

On his travels out of the apartment, Nechama's father once again began to search for another place for the family to hide. Eventually, he learned from a friend that a couple in the little village of Otwock would take Nechama and her sister — again, for a huge sum of money. Plans were made for the girls to travel by train to the village.

At the news that the family was going to be separated the girls were extremely upset, Nechama especially so. But left with no alternative, they knew that they must agree to their parents' wishes.

Arriving in Otwock, Nechama and her sister were relieved by its peaceful isolation. Surrounded by dense forests, Otwock seemed to offer them the protection that they needed. Following the directions that their parents had given them, the girls walked through the village until they came to the address.

A woman named Marta opened the door, and in a cold and distant manner, pointed to two very shy children, introducing them as Jurek and Ania. Nechama looked at the squalor of the place. Marta's home consisted of a kitchen and one large room. In one corner stood a stove and a clothes cabinet. Beds rested in the other three corners. An old wooden table and chairs occupied the center of the room, and over these hung a bare light bulb that cut through the dark and dingy living quarters.

Marta's husband Tosiek was a kind and generous man. Because of his work, he was away from the house from early in the morning until late in the evening. At the sound of his voice, his otherwise sullen children would run to the door and jump into his arms. Much laughter and play followed until the family sat down again to a supper of soup. With Tosiek's arrival, the atmosphere brightened and the tension created by Marta's brooding manner eased.

Because of the family's impoverished circumstances there was little to eat, and Nechama and her sister were constantly hungry. Breakfast consisted of a cup of coffee and a piece of dark bread. After that there was nothing to eat until evening, when a bowl of soup was served.

To fill the empty days, Nechama and her sister took long walks through the village and the surrounding forest. It helped to get away from Marta's gloominess and to share quiet hours and secret thoughts. Occasionally the girls allowed themselves a trip to the bakery to buy a roll with the money their father had given them. On these trips, Nechama and her sister tried not to think of the pain of being separated from their parents, and the knowledge that they might never see them again.

When Nechama's father could risk a visit to Otwock, he would speak of the increasingly desperate situation in Warsaw. He and the girls' mother had been forced to move from one hiding place to another. Hearing this news, Nechama and her sister worried about their parents' safety.

In time, Nechama's father learned of some people in the city of Kielce who, in exchange for money, would find room in their home for the Bawniks. Plans were made for Nechama's sister to go to Kielce with a young man named Wojtek to meet the family. Then Wojtek would go to Warsaw to accompany Nechama's parents to Kielce. Nechama was to stay with Marta and her husband until it was safe enough for her to travel.

On the day that Nechama's father visited her for the

last time in Otwock, he carefully went over the steps that were to be taken. Cautioning her that she must not tell anyone of the family's plans nor of where they were going, he reminded her of the gold and jewelry that had been sewn into her coat. Only in the event of an emergency was Nechama to use any of it. For a brief moment the next morning, Nechama and her father held on to each other. Then, he was gone.

On the day that her father left, Nechama stood at the window and watched him hurry down the street. Tears spilled down her cheeks and her whole body ached with the knowledge that she was alone. She had tried hard not to let her father see her fear and had not allowed herself to cry in his presence.

Nechama missed her sister. Together, they had always been able to give each other support. Now, all of that was changed.

As the days dragged by, the little girl began to wonder if she would ever be reunited with her family. She felt lost and fearful of the future, and longed for the warmth and security of the life she had once lived.

Tosiek sensed Nechama's anxieties and did whatever he could to ease her pain by reassuring her that everything would be all right. Soon, Nechama began to rely on Tosiek's friendship. In the evenings, she would wait for his return and for his fun-loving chatter at the supper table.

One day, after Marta had left the house to go on an errand, Nechama lost her battle with hunger and carved off a thin sliver of bread from a loaf resting on the table. When Marta returned, she immediately discovered the missing piece and accused the child of stealing. Sometime later, Nechama learned how the woman had known that the piece of bread was missing. Along the edge of the loaf, Marta had carved a series of crosses so that if Nechama were to cut off a slice, the crosses would be cut off as well.

After the incident with the bread, Marta's treatment of Nechama turned for the worse. Nothing that the little girl did could please her, and the slightest mistake in the way she did her chores would send the woman into a tirade.

In her loneliness, Nechama began having nightmares about her family. Every night she would dream that her parents and her sister had disappeared and that she would never see them again. And then one wonderful night, Nechama's sister came back to take her to rejoin her parents in Kielce.

The apartment in Kielce consisted of two rooms; in it lived Nechama, her family and eight other people. There was electricity but no running water and no toilet. To get water, Nechama and the others drew from a secluded well. An outhouse in back of the building served as the toilet facility.

In their new hiding place, the presence of Nechama's parents had to be kept secret. The two girls were to act as orphans related to the people with whom they were staying. Nechama and her sister would be the only members of their family to leave the house. In the event of a raid, Nechama's parents would go into a hiding place in the apartment.

Unable to leave the apartment, Nechama's parents tried to find things to do. Nechama's mother kept busy with her cooking, and her husband passed the time reading Russian or Polish classics that the child brought from the library. Reunited with her family, Nechama grew stronger and was soon reading books of her own once again.

As the months of hiding in Kielce passed, the few clothes that the Bawnik family had brought with them became worn and covered with patches. Each owned one pair of shoes, and these had to be resoled many times. But they were together, and that was all that mattered.

The people in Wojtek's family were kind as well as friendly although, like most Polish Christians, they were fiercely anti-Semitic. Nechama was disturbed by their attitude and confused by the fact that despite their feelings, they nevertheless were willing to hide Jews in their home.

In exchange for this protection, Nechama's father had to pay for food for everyone in the apartment and was also responsible for the rent. To get the money, jewelry would be exchanged on the black market. To make the money last, Nechama's father was careful to use it only to fulfill his obligations to Wojtek and his family.

Some time after Nechama and her family had been reunited in Kielce, the Nazis in the city began stepping up their raids. At the beginning, these took place in public areas, but soon the Germans began searching homes as well. It was agreed that in the event of such a raid, Nechama's parents would hide in a storage cellar beneath the floor of the apartment.

Late in 1943, when it became clear that the war was not going well for the Germans, the Polish underground surged with activity, blowing up bridges and trains in and around the city of Warsaw. In return for the sabotage, the Nazis increased the number of their raids and deportations of the Jews. Then came the uprising in the ghetto, where conditions had become desperate. Sickness and disease were out of control and the people were starving. For weeks, the battle raged between the inhabitants of the ghetto and their German captors. In the end, the courageous Jews lost their struggle, the ghetto was sealed, and thousands were sent to extermination camps.

Because of the increased risks of discovery, Nechama and her family, together with some of Wojtek's relatives, who, by Nazi edict, could be executed for hiding Jews, moved to an apartment in the neighborhood that was more secluded, and at once set about building a shelter beneath the floor boards. An old trunk was placed over the shelter to hide the marks where the boards had been cut.

Soon after the family had moved to the new apartment, one of Wojtek's people came to warn them of a raid by the Nazis. Immediately, Nechama's parents rushed to the hiding place and slipped through the tiny opening one at a time. No sooner had Nechama covered the shelter with the trunk, than the Germans rushed into the apartment and began going through closets and checking under beds. As the search continued, one of the Nazis walked over to the area where the trunk lay. Suddenly, Nechama's father coughed.

The soldier stopped and turned in the direction of the cough. Nechama stared at the wall, trying to keep her face free from expression. When no further sound was heard, the German gave the girl a strange little smile, and without mentioning the incident, left with the others.

By 1944, the Bawnik family's funds had begun to run dangerously low. Nechama's father asked Wojtek if he would go to Lublin to recover the little bag that had been given to the German commissioner at the chemical factory for safekeeping, and to pay a visit to Bolek, who had done so much to protect the family. Wojtek agreed to make the trip, and returned soon after with the money, and a warm letter from the commissioner, conveying his joy that the Bawniks were still alive.

But despite their gratitude to the German for returning their money, the Bawniks were deeply saddened by Wojtek's news of Bolek's tragic death following a Gestapo raid on his apartment. Bolek had been arrested, along with several Jews who had been in hiding there. Others had been shot to death. Imprisoned and unable to contact the German officer who had protected him for so long, Bolek had been given the choice of death by torture or suicide. Within a short time, he had taken his own life with a rope that had been left on his cell bed.

In January of 1945, the Germans in Poland were pushed back farther and farther by the advancing Russian army. With each passing day, the Bawnik family's hopes of survival increased.

And then one night, the Allied bombings began. Nechama and her sister, along with their parents, who had not left their hiding place for what seemed like an eternity, raced to an air raid shelter. There, huddled together, they waited out the night.

At daybreak the next morning, the bombings stopped and all was quiet. Returning to the apartment, Nechama and her family caught sight of the first Russian soldiers moving down the street. The long ordeal was over at last.

City in Flames

Before the bombs fell, Königsberg was a lovely old city, Karla Poewe's mother once said. She described the grace of the river Pregel as it wandered past beautiful old buildings steeped in history, the swans on the castle pond, the promenade and the confectioners' shops with their little cafe tables crowded with people.

In the afternoons, there were excursions through the city on the electric streetcars, and puppet theaters and concerts for the children. In the evenings, there were more concerts for the adults and much entertaining among friends. A cultural life like this could help one forget what was happening to one's country and its people.

Karla's home, located on the river Pregel, was filled with women. Her father, Hugo, a kind and cheerful man, was away at war. Older than her mother by twenty years, Hugo Poewe had been a successful German businessman before being summoned for compulsory military service. In addition to Karla and her mother, there was Gudi, her younger sister; Bertha, the cook; Hedwig, the housekeeper; and Aunt Trudi, the girls' nanny.

Karla's mother was a small, beautiful young woman. An affectionate and caring parent, she spent much time with her children, taking them on walks and weaving the most wonderful fairy tales as they meandered along the river front.

And then, suddenly, in the winter of 1945, Königsberg was in flames. As bombs rained down from the sky, buildings turned to rubble and the women and children of the city took to the streets. Karla and Gudi found themselves swept up by their mother and Aunt Trudi, and together the four raced to the castle pond. Near the water's edge they stood hand in hand, choking on the suffocating air about them, ready to jump if they had to. Better to drown than to burn to death. Minutes later, the two women changed their minds, grabbed the children and joined a crowd of people running toward an air raid shelter. From every direction came the sounds of rushing feet, the shattering of glass and stone, and the thunder of planes overhead.

For days, the bombings continued. Around her in a

crowded basement shelter, Karla listened to the sobbing of the old people. As she huddled next to her
mother and the others, she heard her own voice rise
with the screams of the children. There was no food,
no water, no sleep. Only the deafening noise, the
blinding light and the crush of buildings collapsing.

Sometimes, during a lull, Karla's mother or Aunt
Trudi would go into the streets to find something to
eat. Eventually, they and the children learned to survive on sorrel, tree bark or a rare crust of a black bun.
Karla's mother had a friend who was a pharmacist.
From her, she was able to get some cod liver oil. But it
was not enough. Somehow, they would have to find a
way out of the city. The train to Dresden was the only
answer.

The train moved slowly through the countryside.
Karla, Gudi, her mother and Aunt Trudi were among
the passengers who had jammed themselves into every
available seat and space, traveling for hours through
the darkness in the hope of reaching Dresden. At day-
light, the train stopped and everyone ran to the bushes
to relieve themselves. Then back on the train, back to
the hunger and fear.

The passengers on the train lost all sense of time and

place. As the bombings continued, they found themselves moving forward and backward, shunted from
one train track to another to avoid being hit, stopping
and then starting again, lumbering through the deso-
lation that lay about them. Sometimes, the train idled
on the tracks for hours.

After many days, the passengers heard that they
were at last nearing Dresden, the one great German
city that had remained untouched by Allied attack. A
center of history and art and treasures of the past, it
was believed by many to be the safest of places, a national air raid shelter, the people called it.

On the night of February 13, 1945, less than three
months before the end of the war, Dresden was hit. As
the train carrying Karla and the others approached
the outskirts of the city, the bombs began to fall. Ex-
plosions and fires followed. The train came to a halt,
moved again, then stopped again. Once more, the
changing to another track. Once more, the endless
journey in the opposite direction.

That night, and in the days that followed, more
than 35,000 people lost their lives as firestorms consumed one of Europe's most beautiful cities, and some
of the greatest art treasures in the world.

* * *

The train moved southward to Netzchkau, near the city of Plauen. Karla Poewe and her family found shelter in another crowded basement. Wrapped in her blanket, the little girl listened as her mother tried to comfort her with a fairy tale. Outside, a convoy of trucks could be heard passing through the street. Karla's mother stood and parted a covering over the window just wide enough to see tall, dark soldiers riding on their carriers. The Americans were arriving.

Years later, Karla remembered that basement in Netzschkau. The darkness, the stench and the moans of the dying. As bodies were removed, others replaced them on the floor. Each day, Karla's mother and Aunt Trudi would go into the streets to forage for food, leaving the two children in the care of a cousin. Karla, four and a half years old at the time, had stopped speaking.

After weeks in Netzschkau, Karla's mother received a letter from her husband and learned that he had been taken prisoner by the advancing Russians. On the slightest chance that his release might eventually bring him to Netzschkau, she knew that she had to wait for him. But conditions at the shelter had become intolerable and disease was spreading. Desperate for the safety of her children, Karla's mother made the painful decision to place her children in a Catholic orphanage near Berlin. Despite the weeks and perhaps months that they would be separated from one another, the orphanage offered the only hope for her children's survival. There was no other choice.

Several lonely months were to pass before Karla and her sister could be reunited with their mother. During that time, the Allied bombings continued and the two little girls spent many nights huddled together in the basement of the orphanage with all of the other children. But the nuns were kind, and did their best to care for their charges. Each day, more children would arrive, and food and medical supplies grew scarce.

On the eighth of May, 1945, the war in Europe came to an end, and within a short time, Karla and her sister and mother were together once again. But during the months of separation, Karla had grown thin and frail. Food held no interest for her and she continued to find it impossible to speak. Not knowing what to do for the child, Karla's mother sent her to stay with her grandmother, who had found shelter in the British sector near Hamburg, where a few potatoes were available along with a little bread, and refugees could find a room here and there. (After the war, the Allies divided Germany into two sections. Hamburg became part of West Germany, which was occupied by British and American troops. Netzschkau, where Karla had been living, was in East Germany, which was controlled by the Russians.)

Karla's grandmother, whom she called Omi, was a woman of great wisdom and faith. A devout Catholic who had given birth to six sons and a number of daughters, she was fiercely independent. Raised on a farm near the Russian border of East Prussia, she had had no time for Adolf Hitler, "that lackey from Austria," as she called him during his rise to power.

With Omi's loving care, Karla grew stronger each day. When she had difficulty swallowing her food, Omi would play singing games with her and teach her to say little rhymes.

Each Sunday, and sometimes in between, Karla walked to the Catholic church with Omi. Afterward, they would visit the Gypsies and Omi would have her fortune read. A strong believer in both Jesus and the cards, the old woman would ask the Gypsies about her six handsome sons who been called up to fight in Hitler's war.

Karla's grandmother was a great storyteller like her daughter. But instead of fairy tales, Omi created her own stories that took Karla to mythical worlds beyond worlds. A walk in the woods could turn into a magic carpet. With these stories, the little girl's fears diminished, if only for moments at a time.

As summer drew to a close, Omi and Karla worked on the local farms to gather the harvest. In return, the farmers would give them scraps of vegetables that could not be sold in the marketplace. Corn husks would be dried and pounded into a crude flour, from which Omi would make thick soups and little pancakes.

With Omi, Karla learned to forage in the meadows, gathering dandelion and lime tree leaves. Berries would be found in season, and wild plums and hazelnuts. When acorns fell from the giant oaks, the old woman and the little girl would take them to the pig farmers and receive bits of food in exchange. Life with Omi gave balance to Karla's world. One worked hard, and received something for that work. And in between the work, there were Omi's songs and stories and fragments of peace amidst the rubble of the war's remains.

After several months with Omi, Karla grew stronger and went back to live with her mother and sister Gudi, who had moved into two rooms which they shared with an older woman in the village of Werdau, in East

Germany. While Karla's mother went foraging for food, the little girl would walk by the river with a doll that her mother had made out of remnants of material she had found.

One day as Karla was walking, a child approached her and stared longingly at the doll.

"If you let me play with your doll, I'll give you a doll carriage," she said. Karla nodded her head, handing the doll to the little girl.

Each day for some time, the girls would meet and Karla would hand her doll to the other child, expecting to see the carriage that had been promised. But the carriage never appeared. Finally, as the child was leaving one morning, Karla tried to follow her, but was outrun.

Later, Karla found the girl living in one of several bombed-out buildings on a hill. Few windows remained and doors opened onto filth and emptiness. From one of the buildings the little girl emerged, and came toward Karla. Her dress was ragged and torn and her face was smudged with dirt. As they talked, Karla discovered the truth about the child. Her father had been killed in the war, and her sister and brother were dead as well. Her mother was in an insane asylum. And there was no doll carriage.

As the months went by, Karla grew sickly again, and

an aunt was summoned to take her back to Omi. On a warm summer day, Karla and her aunt set out on their journey. Changing vehicles several times, they finally found a bus that took them close to the border of the Russian sector. Karla and her aunt walked slowly and cautiously to the barrier where a Russian soldier stood guard, because it had now become extremely difficult to leave East Germany and cross into the West, where Omi lived.

The barrier was lowered and Karla's aunt was asked to hand over their identification papers. Examining them, the guard told them they would have to wait.

In a nearby wooded area, the two spotted a large crowd of people being herded together by a number of Russian soldiers. Shots were fired, and many of the people fell to the ground. Those who remained standing were taken away.

The guard at the barrier gate was called away to assist with the new prisoners. Looking down at Karla, he smiled, and hurriedly thrust the papers back into Karla's aunt's hands. Just as quickly, he left. As the woman and child stood waiting at the barrier, a voice called to them. Looking around, they saw a German soldier sitting alone on a rock.

"What are you waiting for?" the soldier whispered.

"You have your papers. For heaven's sake, move on!"

Karla's aunt hesitated, wondering whether she should listen to the man.

"If you walk fast, you can catch the bus," the soldier continued. "Do you want to go to Siberia like those people over there?"

Rushing away from the Soviet barrier, Karla's aunt pulled her along the road until they saw the bus approaching. When it didn't appear to be slowing down, the woman ran to the middle of the road and forced the bus to stop. The door burst open and the driver shouted that his bus was full. But Karla's aunt stood her ground, protesting that if he didn't take the child and her they would be killed by the Russians. With this, the bus driver gave in and allowed the woman and child to stay. As the vehicle moved slowly down the road, Karla and her aunt heard a shot. Looking back, they saw the German soldier lying on the road beside the Russian check point.

One day, Karla's grandmother took her to see her aunt, who had found a place to live nearby. There was someone she was about to meet, Omi said cheerfully as the two walked along the street.

Arriving at her aunt's, Karla found herself standing in front of a tall, frail-looking man with dark circles under his eyes. The man was Karla's father.

On May 20, 1948, after nine months in a hospital, Karla's father died. Her mother had waited for his return since 1943 when, like many other older men, he had been called up to replace the thousands of soldiers whose deaths had inflicted heavy losses on the German army. Imprisoned by the Russians toward the end of the war, he became gravely ill, and when it was certain that he was going to die, he was released.

During the months that followed the death of Karla's father, Frau Poewe tried repeatedly to get identification papers that would allow her to take her children west to the British sector in Buxtehude, not far from Hamburg. Day after day, she went to the Russian authorities to ask for the papers, and each time she was refused.

To support her family, Karla's mother, who had once loved the theater and the arts and beautiful parties, took a job selling ice cream at a nearby entertainment park. And then one day after months of delay, the identification papers came through.

Overjoyed, Frau Poewe lost no time in packing the few clothes the family now owned, and the three set out on their journey northward. Since few buses or trolleys were running and trains carrying refugees were overloaded, the mother and her two little girls walked most of the way. Karla and Gudi each had little bundles to carry; their mother carried an old piece of luggage she had found.

In order to avoid the crowds, the three usually traveled at night, stopping occasionally to rest and forage for food. Karla's feet hurt as she and Gudi walked along but she didn't complain. The three of them were safe and they were together. And as she looked into her mother's eyes she could see that they were bright and full of hope.

Finally, on October 1, 1948, Karla and her mother and Gudi arrived at the checkpoint leading into the British sector. Their papers were stamped and they were each given tea. It was warm and sweet.

At first, Karla and her mother and sister lived in a single room in Buxtehude with Omi and another aunt. The two girls slept in a closet and the three women used the bed. But after a time, Omi moved out to find a room of her own and Karla's mother found work that enabled her to rent three rooms in the city of Hamburg. One big room held a large stove and was used as a kitchen, dining room, and living room. The other two rooms served as bedrooms. For the first time since they had left Königsberg, Karla and her sister had a room of their own.

One day, Karla and Gudi prepared for their first day of school. They were excited but frightened. Because of the war and their years of traveling from one place to another, they had never been able to attend classes.

After school that afternoon, Karla stood waiting for Gudi to come out of the building. A group of students gathered around her and began teasing her because she was so big for her class. Then the children began pointing their fingers at her, calling her "Flüchtling, Flüchtling!" A refugee, a refugee . . .

In Herr Broden's class, Karla struggled to shape her letters in just the right way. And when called upon, she could only whisper her answers. When she remained silent, she received a rap on the knuckles with the teacher's pointing stick.

During the arithmetic lessons, Herr Broden would assign a set of problems to the students and then sit back to play the violin, which was always on his desk. A severe and withdrawn man with a faraway look in his eyes, Herr Broden was at once frightening and puzzling. But when he played his violin, his whole countenance changed and his melodies were soft and beautiful.

One morning in class, Herr Broden discovered that his stick had been broken and demanded to know who had done it. No one answered. Again, the teacher challenged the students. Finally, when Karla became upset with the repeated questioning, Herr Broden came to the conclusion that it was she who had broken the stick. Called to the front of the room, Karla was told to bend over, and when she did so, she was struck repeatedly with the broken stick.

Throughout the morning Karla had to remain standing with her face to the wall. The class giggled. She was angry and humiliated. In her fright, she could not even use her voice to defend herself.

Later that day, a boy in the class stood up and admitted to Herr Broden that he had broken the stick. With that, the teacher ordered the boy to stand in another corner. Yet despite the boy's confession, Karla was not released from her position at the wall until school was dismissed.

That evening, Karla told her mother what had happened in school. The next morning, she was too ill to attend class.

When Karla was able to return to school, her mother accompanied her and had a conference with the principal and Herr Broden. As the little girl stood aside listening, her mother explained all that had happened to her children during the war and asked Herr Broden to be more understanding of her daughter.

In the weeks that followed, Karla found out why Herr Broden behaved the way he did. Years before, during the bombing of Dresden, Herr Broden had witnessed the deaths of his wife and daughter. As bombs continued to fall on the city, the two had panicked and run out into the streets. Herr Broden ran after them, only to watch them consumed by the flames of the firestorms.

In the principal's office one morning, Karla was introduced to a kind-looking man with bright, friendly eyes and a warm smile. His name was Herr Deckwerth, and he was to be her new teacher.

"There is someone I want you to meet," Herr Deckwerth told Karla. "It's my son. You and he must spend some time together."

After school, Karla walked with Herr Deckwerth to

his home. There, she met his wife, a beautiful woman with long dark hair braided into a double ring about her head. The atmosphere in the home was happy and loving.

Moments later, Karla met Benjamin, the couple's son. Coming into the room slowly on thin, weak legs encased in heavy braces, the boy struggled to put one foot in front of the other. As he approached his father eagerly, he spoke a garble of unintelligible words. But the lights in his eyes were full of love.

When the boy reached his father, Karla was told that he was nine, the same age as she. A victim of polio, he was badly crippled, Herr Deckwerth explained, but despite his handicaps Benjamin wanted to learn how to do things himself.

Karla's new teacher asked his son if he wanted to try to walk toward her. Benjamin turned and labored toward her, and at last reached the place where she was standing. Just as the boy was about to fall, Karla caught him. The boy laughed and spoke several incoherent words to her, and Karla suddenly started to speak out loud for the first time in years. Herr Deckwerth hugged his wife, and Karla couldn't believe how happy and safe she felt.

* * *

Karla visited Benjamin Deckwerth three times a week. With each visit, she would help him to practice his walking. Then, she would put objects in the boy's hands and tell him how to say their names. Gradually, the boy's legs grew stronger and he was able to speak more clearly. And all the time, Karla kept talking, hearing the sounds of her own voice as she spoke to her new and very special friend.

In class with Herr Deckwerth, Karla learned to paint pictures. Soon, she began to create scenes that were remarkable for their beauty. Herr Deckwerth praised her work, and in time, the paintings began to draw the attention of her classmates and other teachers.

One day, Karla drew a picture that pleased her teacher so much that he decided to enter it in a contest sponsored by UNICEF, the United Nations organization that worked in behalf of the world's children. Karla's painting won first prize in the contest and it was later exhibited in more than forty countries around the world.

In class, the little girl learned to write poems and to recite them aloud. These, too, showed promise and were entered into school contests. On the day of the dedication of the rebuilding of her school, Karla was chosen to recite the poem that she had written for the ceremony.

As she walked to the podium, she stood before the microphone and looked out onto an audience crowded with parents and school children. Karla's legs felt weak and a shudder went through her. Would she be able to speak?

The people waited in silence for the young girl to begin. Seconds passed. And then, as if from a distance, Karla heard her voice, high and unnatural at first but gradually gaining in strength and fluidity.

"The nightingale is very ugly," Omi would always say, "but when it sings it melts our hearts." That day, Karla Poewe was the nightingale. The only difference was that, unlike the lonely songster of the night, she had grown quite beautiful indeed.

Sea Watch

Several miles north of Scotland, a group of islands known as the Orkneys stretch out in a ragged path across the waters of the Atlantic. Thousands of years ago ancient tribes built mysterious stone formations, underground burial chambers, and houses complete with adjoining passageways, stone beds, and fireplaces. In the ninth century, Norsemen from Norway and Denmark arrived, settling into the Orkneys and its neighboring islands, the Shetlands, for five hundred years.

Ringed by rugged cliffs, quiet coves, and harbors, the Orkneys are home to hundreds of species of birds. In the springtime, seals bask on low-lying rocks at the edge of the sea. The Orkneys, despite their northerly location, have a relatively mild climate due to the influence of Gulf Stream currents.

At the beginning of World War II, the period known in Britain as the Phony War, German planes swept across the skies above the Orkneys, and submarines moved soundlessly through the surrounding waters. To most of the islanders, it seemed clear that Hitler was planning to invade the British Isles.

By late summer of 1939, events were moving quickly. After Hitler's invasion of Poland on September 1, Prime Minister Neville Chamberlain appointed Winston Churchill to the Cabinet as First Lord of the Admiralty. Two days later, after the sinking of the British passenger ship *Athenia,* Parliament declared war on Germany.

From September of 1939 to May of 1940, sixteen-year-old Bessie Shea kept a diary of events as they occurred, and of her experiences and feelings about the progress of the war. From her farm home on an island called Mainland, Bessie wrote of air raids over the nearby capital town of Kirkwall and of attacks on the naval base at Scapa Flow.

Bessie's story began with the sighting of the first German submarine on September 5, 1940. On that same day, three enemy spies were caught on her island. The next day, as she was taking the cattle out of the barn, she heard the sound of aircraft. Looking up, she spotted nineteen antiaircraft shells exploding over Kirkwall.

In her next entry, Bessie noted the capture of two German ships. One ship was sunk and the crews of both vessels were taken prisoner. Three seamen managed to escape, however, slipping away in a motor boat. Two of the islanders gave chase, discovering the Germans the next morning in the harbor of a neighboring island. Pulling up alongside the Germans, the islanders found them to be friendly and offered them cigarettes and a pot of tea while waiting for an armed British patroller to pick them up. But before the young Germans got their tea, the patroller arrived and took them aboard at gunpoint.

With the arrival of October, Britain initiated bombing raids on German naval bases, sank its first enemy submarine, and sent expeditionary forces into Dunkirk, France. Hitler, in the meantime, was threatening to bomb every civilian town in Britain and to sink every ship in the Royal Navy. In her diary, Bessie recorded the visits to Kirkwall and to Scapa Flow by King George and Winston Churchill, who had ordered that additional antiaircraft artillery be posted along Mainland's shores.

Summer, with its rumors of an impending invasion and its accompanying anxieties, had come to an end.

With it came Bessie's realization that the activities she had so enjoyed — the dances and Bible class trips — would be a thing of the past for a long time.

On October 14, the Germans conducted a massive air raid on the naval base at nearby Scapa Flow, sinking the *Royal Oak,* the country's most powerful ship. In the attack, more than eight hundred young seamen in training lost their lives.

During the following month, the Germans began bombing the Shetlands, and a spy who had reportedly been poisoning the water supply was captured on the island of Flotta. Later, Bessie noted that three German seamen, adrift without food or water for several days, had been captured near Fife.

By mid-November, air raids throughout the Orkneys were a common occurrence, and naval battles in the North Atlantic had begun. Bessie and her family had learned to recognize the sounds of German war planes as they flew over Kirkwall and Scapa Flow, a clacking noise very different from the drone of Britain's aircraft.

As the days progressed, however, the routines of everyday life changed little. The cattle still had to be milked and farm chores completed. In the local shops, food was still plentiful.

On the twenty-second of the month, as the clack-

clacking of an enemy aircraft approached, Bessie grabbed the family binoculars and ran outside. As she fixed her sights, she saw a broad-winged monoplane with a black cross on its side. The plane flew overhead, passed southward, then turned and circled above her head. Minutes later the plane was over Kirkwall, and antiaircraft guns blasted away while a British destroyer took up the chase.

During the last week of November, as the battle in the North Atlantic grew more intense, debris from sunken ships drifted onto the beaches at Scapa Flow. One morning, Bessie wrote that she had found "a good box." Later that afternoon she returned to the beach to find a wooden plank and what she called "some oddments."

In her walks along the beach, Bessie frequently spotted the periscopes of German submarines rising above the water. She had also learned that listening posts for enemy aircraft had been set in place throughout the Orkneys.

On December 3, Bessie recounted an adventure that gave her cause to believe that "not all Germans [were] bad." In her diary, the young girl noted that an enemy submarine had just torpedoed a British ship, forcing her crew to take to their lifeboats. As the vessel sank into the sea, the submarine surfaced, opened its hatch, and offered hot food and drinks to the crewmen, who by now were soaked and shivering in the bitter Atlantic winds. Then, keeping a close watch, the Germans waited until a British destroyer approached to rescue the seamen. As the submarine moved off, the ship's commander called out, "Tell Churchill that there's still *some* humanity!"

On December 17, Canadian troops started to arrive in Britain, and air training went into full force. One week later, the first squadron of Australian airmen received their assignments.

The war effort was well under way by January 1940, and government rationing of butter, meat, bacon, and sugar went into effect. Belgium and the Netherlands prepared for the inevitable German invasion. At the same time, Bessie and many other Orcadians were convinced that they, too, were about to be invaded.

On January 22, an entry in Bessie's diary noted the rumored evacuation of all schoolchildren in the town of Kirkwall and the eventual evacuation of all women and children from throughout the Orkneys.

In her diary entry for the following day, Bessie wrote that she had attended her Guild meeting, where there was much discussion among the members regarding evacuation plans. These plans, she later learned, were proven to be false. In her final comments that evening, Bessie wrote of the sinking of a British tanker at nearby Inganess Bay. As the air war increased over the islands, additional antiaircraft batteries were installed on the neighboring island of Shapinsay, along with more than one hundred men and officers to operate them.

On the last day of January, 1940, three ships were sunk near Scapa Flow, where thousands of men and women were now stationed at the naval base. Two of the vessels were destroyers and the third was a coast guard patrol boat. Many lives were lost during the attack, and one body from the sinkings was found on the beach near Sandgarth.

That same day, Bessie wrote that she continued to discover fragments of wood along the shore, and that new antiaircraft installations would be arriving in Stromberry, along with a searchlight.

Less than a week later, three more bodies were washed ashore, and a single German plane fired on the ship *Rota*, inflicting only slight damage. The aircraft then proceeded on to the neighboring island of Shapinsay, bombing an armed fishing trawler. Coast guard patrols moved in to defend the trawler as the plane circled and finally flew off.

Bessie found a 100-pound keg of Danish butter on the beach on February 10. The wood was water-soaked and fragile but otherwise untouched. Walking a bit farther, she spotted an empty cask. As Bessie was making her discoveries, two German submarines were sunk in nearby waters.

Several days later, one of the war's first mass rescues took place far to the north in a Norwegian fjord, when 299 British prisoners of war from the HMS *Cossack* were taken from the German warship *Altmark* and brought to safety.

On the evening of March 16, while Bessie was shopping in the village, the sounds of enemy aircraft approached. Running out of the store with a friend, she counted more than a dozen German fighters in a sky emblazoned with fire from both the aircraft and artillery guns from the British fleet at Scapa Flow harbor. Suddenly, a tremendous flash broke out in the waters near Kirkwall. Then, nine planes from the squadron broke away and headed for the northern area of the island. From another direction came the roar of additional enemy fighter planes.

During a momentary lull in the action, Bessie raced for home. As she reached the village of Newhouse, the skies were lit by flashes of fire from the town of Stromness, "lighting up the west Mainland hills brilliantly," as Bessie recorded in her diary. Sixteen search-lights swept through the darkness as antiaircraft shells blasted overhead. The smell of gunpowder filled the air and shrapnel fell from every direction as the girl struggled to reach her farmhouse. Soon the planes moved off into the distance, and all was strangely quiet once again.

Bessie described in depth the bombing of the Scapa Flow Naval Base and the blowing up of the Bridge of Waithe in her diary the following day. In that action, a battleship was severely damaged, along with seven cottages in the village of Stromness. Seven people were injured and one life was lost. All-out war had come to the Orkneys. In his regular broadcast over the wireless radio late that evening, the Nazi sympathizer known and ridiculed as Lord Haw Haw reveled in the damages that had been inflicted on the islands, reporting that the German raids had been successful and that none of Germany's planes had been lost.

Enemy action in the waters surrounding the islands was on the increase. Bessie wrote of an attack on a British naval convoy and the damaging of three destroyers. A fourth had to be scuttled.

Despite all of the events that were unfolding, the people on Mainland and on the other Orkney islands tried to get on with their lives. Bessie excitedly described the dress rehearsal for a village concert and one of the participants' difficulty in speaking plainly enough to be heard. Another in the group caught the measles and had to be replaced. A dance had been scheduled and a number of the newly arrived Territorials (soldiers of the volunteer reserve forces) were expected to attend. A friend had gone to the village of Stromness to see the houses that had been bombed. The Bridge of Waithe was salvageable. The concert was a success and Bessie's recitation "good."

The Territorials installed a searchlight at the Elwickbank Park as well as additional antiaircraft guns on March 25. The trucks carrying the machinery passed Bessie's farm. The convoy moved down the road, the soldiers waved cheerfully at Bessie, and she waved back. Later, the girl's mother showed her displeasure with her daughter's behavior by not allowing her to attend a dance the men gave shortly after.

Two days later, Bessie noted in her diary that Miss Balfour, the spinster who lived in the nearby castle, had issued orders that the Territorials billeted with her would not be permitted to eat their meals inside, so the soldiers had to set up their portable stoves on the tennis court and "eat there in the rain!" In addition,

the men were told to remove their boots before entering the building. Their lieutenant, however, was
served *his* meals inside.

The German air raids over the Orkneys continued
without let-up. At dusk one evening, tracer bullets
scanned the skies overhead and searchlights on the islands of Shapinsay and Mainland shot upward, moving
swiftly across the heavens as the aircraft approached.
Suddenly, there was a tremendous thunder of firepower. The countryside was illuminated by shells and
bullets exploding and guns from the batteries sent
brilliant flashes into the air. Bessie counted thirty-
seven searchlight beams. While the action continued,
she shouted encouragement, marching around excitedly outside of the farmhouse and whistling an old
British nursery tune.

On April 8, the British destroyer *Glow-worm* was
sunk off the coast of Norway after colliding with a
German cruiser. Several days later, Germany invaded
Denmark, and landed successfully in five strategic
Norwegian coastal cities.

At 8:30 one evening, the skies above Bessie's village
were alive once again with firepower. Kirkwall was
under attack. Air raid sirens sounded their warning,
and searchlights above all of the surrounding villages

went to work. As Bessie and her family watched, the lights centered on a huge aircraft, a four-engine bomber, roaring overhead with its tailguns firing. In the bay close to the village, an armed trawler fired back in defense.

On May 10, 1940, as the Germans invaded the Netherlands, Belgium, Luxembourg, and France, Winston Churchill replaced the ineffective Neville Chamberlain as Prime Minister. Bessie Shea reported the dropping of hundreds of enemy parachutes over Holland and Belgium, and expressed her dismay that all of Norway with the exception of the port at Narvik had been lost.

Several days later, an officer from the searchlight battery patrol spotted an enemy submarine cruising through the bay at the Scapa Flow Naval Base during the night. German planes carrying paratroopers ready for a jump over Mainland had been intercepted by British fighter planes in hot pursuit. Following this action, the Territorials brought in additional forces and antiaircraft batteries.

On May 20, Winston Churchill delivered the first of many brilliant addresses that served to inspire hope and courage in the hearts and minds of the British people: "I speak to you for the first time as prime minister in a solemn hour for the life of our country, of our empire, of our allies, and above all, of the call of freedom . . ."

In her diary that evening, Bessie noted, "The war gets more serious. I can hear heavy firing in the east, but cannot see anything." At the moment of her writing, the Germans had captured the historic cities of Abbeville and Amiens in France, and were pushing toward the English Channel at Noyelles.

In the entry which followed, Bessie made mention of several "very vivid dreams" that she had had during the previous night. In each, she saw "quarries and water." Later that same day, she wrote of a curious coincidence, noting, "a case of suicide or accidental drowning occurred in Sands."

Bessie Shea's final diary recording was made on May 25, 1940. In it, she reported that the Germans had broken through the French lines of defense and had captured Boulogne. "I didn't hear the nine o'clock news last night but the news is getting worse and worse. What if Hitler wins? He can't. *In all human reason he can't.*"

Hitler's forces penetrated deep into the heart of France until the British Expeditionary Forces and their Allies had retreated to the coast at Dunkirk, where, between May 26 and June 4, the massive evacuation of

338,226 men took place. On that day, a defiant Winston Churchill addressed the House of Commons: "We shall go on to the end. We shall fight in France, we shall fight on the seas and oceans . . . We shall fight on the landing grounds, we shall fight in the fields and in the streets, we shall fight in the hills: We shall never surrender."

The war in Britain and Europe steadily worsened. On the first of July, 217 Allied merchant ships were sunk by German submarines in an effort to take control of the Atlantic, and on the tenth of that month, the first heavy bombing of British and Welsh docks took place, marking the beginning of the Battle of Britain.

By late August, the first bombs fell on central London, and on September 1, the London Blitz on civilians had begun in earnest.

In the months that lay ahead, Adolf Hitler continued to score victory after victory in Europe, and it appeared possible that Bessie Shea's fears of an invasion would be realized. But that was not to be. By the following May, the Germans' relentless bombings suddenly stopped. The courage and steadfast resolve of the British people had sent a clear message to the Germans. The Battle of Britain had been won, and the Germans never did land on British soil.

Endless Night

Tucked into the mountains of Romania, there is a peaceful little town called Sighet. In the surrounding countryside, rivers and streams wind in and out of ancient hamlets where peasants tend their fields much as they have for centuries. With the coming of spring, the air is filled with the freshness of the season and gardens come to life in a blaze of color.

Here in Sighet, a young boy named Elie Wiesel once lived with his parents and three sisters. Elie's father was a merchant and a leader of the predominantly Jewish community. His mother was a well-educated woman whose life was centered around the teachings of the Hebrew scriptures.

Elie Wiesel was a serious child with a thirst for learning. At an early age, he began studying the Torah and immersed himself in the rituals and prayers of the Hasidic faith. Unlike other boys in his neighborhood, he preferred the synagogue to the playground.

On holy days, Elie's grandfather, Dodye Feig, visited the family for the ceremonial feasts and the services at the synagogue. Elie loved these visits because his grandfather was a remarkable storyteller who brought to life the Hebrew legends of the ancient past. In Sighet, the seasons came and went undisturbed, and the people remained untouched by the clouds of war that hung over much of Europe. And then, suddenly, everything changed.

In 1942, the police who were in charge of Sighet and its neighboring communities ordered the arrest and deportation of all Jews who had not been born in Romania. Among those was a wise little man known to everyone as Moshe the Beadle.

Elie Wiesel loved Moshe the Beadle, for it was he who had introduced him to the great books of the Hebrew scriptures called the cabbala, which sought to explain the mysteries of the Hebrew teachings.

On the day of the deportation, the people of Sighet followed Moshe and the other Jews who were being deported to the train station. Carrying sacks of food, they presented them to their departing neighbors and wept as the people were herded into cattle cars for destinations unknown. Elie watched as the trains left the station and he, too, wept.

Months passed and life in Sighet returned to normal. In the marketplace, food was plentiful, and in the streets the children carried out their ritual games.

And then one evening as Elie was about to enter the synagogue, he saw Moshe the Beadle. Elie was stunned by the man's appearance and by the story he had to tell.

As the train carrying Moshe and the others crossed the Hungarian border and moved into German-occupied Polish territory, the Gestapo boarded the cars and ordered everyone out. Near the station platform, a long line of open trucks awaited the prisoners. Shouting at the people and pushing them along with their rifle butts, the Gestapo shoved the prisoners into the trucks and drove them into a dense forest.

Finally, the trucks stopped and again the people were ordered to get out. Brandishing their rifles, the Gestapo tossed shovels at the crowd and told them to dig. For hours the people struggled with their work. When they had finished, the soldiers started firing. Again and again, the shots rang through the forest as the people fell into the mass grave that they themselves had dug. Moshe was wounded in the leg and fell with the others, praying that the soldiers would believe him dead.

For a long time, Moshe lay quietly amidst the bodies that had fallen around and on top of him. Then, when the last truck had left the site of the slaughter, he climbed out of the ditch and hobbled slowly through the trees, leaving behind him his family, his children, and his friends.

Why, Elie asked, had Moshe the Beadle returned to Sighet?

To warn the people, the little man answered. Terrible things were happening and the citizens of Sighet were no longer safe.

Day after day, Moshe the Beadle told his story of the massacre in the forest. He spoke to men and women in the factories and the synagogues and even in the marketplace. But the people refused to listen. Nothing like that could possibly have happened. Poor old Moshe had gone mad.

In the evenings, the people gathered around their radios to listen to the news from London. In Germany, British and American war planes were targeting major cities and blowing up ammunitions works. Hitler had lost the battle of Stalingrad. There was even talk of a major offensive. Soon, the people said, it would be all over.

By the middle of 1943, the hard-fought campaign in North Africa was drawing to a close. By May, General Rommel, "The Desert Fox," and his German forces had surrendered.

In April of the following year, as the warmth of spring returned to Sighet and the trees were bursting with buds, the Germans marched into Hungary. Three days later, German soldiers swept through the streets of Sighet.

At first, little happened. German officers established themselves in hotels and homes throughout the town. They ate in the coffee shops, shopped in the stores and bought fruit in the marketplace. No shots were fired. No one was threatened. And the Jews of Sighet continued to believe that no harm would come to them.

With the approach of Passover week, the people busied themselves with their preparations. Houses were cleaned from top to bottom. Fresh curtains were hung at the windows and books were taken outdoors for a dusting. The women readied the traditional foods for the Seder and the men gathered in prayer in their homes since orders had been issued for the closing of the synagogues.

During the week-long festivities, the people ate and drank and gave thanks that they had been spared.

On the seventh day of Passover, the leaders of the Jewish community were arrested by the Germans and all of the others were forbidden to leave their homes for three days. Anyone who did so would be shot. In addition, all gold and jewelry was to be turned over to the police.

Next came the orders that all Jews were to wear a yellow star on their clothing. The people could no longer eat in restaurants, use public transportation, or leave their homes after the curfew at six in the evening.

Shortly after, the Germans blocked off two sections of the town and established ghettos where all of the Jews of Sighet were to be confined. Since Elie's home was inside one of these sections, he and his family were not required to move like most of the other Jews in Sighet. But because the house was located on one of the corners of the new ghetto, all windows facing the outside street were sealed. Relatives who had been driven from their homes in other parts of the town moved in with the Wiesels. The two ghettos were ringed by barbed wire.

For a time, the people felt safe. And for the next several weeks, the situation remained quiet. Elie and some of the other boys took their studies of the Talmud to a little park where they worked in the warmth of the spring sun.

Then one evening, just as dusk was falling, a man came into the courtyard where Elie and his father and a few others had gathered. Something was happening. The Gestapo had been seen patroling the ghetto, and a special meeting of the Jewish Council had been called. Elie's father, a member of the council, left immediately with the messenger.

As the hours dragged by, people in the ghetto crowded into the courtyard. At midnight, Elie's father returned with the dreaded news. Both ghettos in Sighet were to be liquidated and the people deported. Each person would be permitted to take a sack of clothing and food enough to last for the journey. The people listened in silence.

Later that night, one of Elie's relatives rushed into the room where he and his parents and sisters were trying to sleep. Someone had been heard knocking on one of the windows that faced the outside of the ghetto. A warning, perhaps? A Christian offering a place to hide? But by the time everyone reached the window, the person had fled.

At dawn the next day, Elie and his family buried what they could of the family treasures: his mother, the silver candelabra that she used on the eve of Shabbat each week; his father, the savings of a lifetime. Elie's older sisters buried what things they could near the cellar; Elie and his younger sister, Tzipora, worked in the garden under a tall poplar tree. Elie buried the gold watch he had been given less than two years before in honor of his bar mitzvah. Tzipora hid a favorite toy.

By eight o'clock in the morning, the police were swarming in the streets, banging on doors and shouting to the people to empty their houses. Soon, everyone was standing outside with their sacks of clothing and food.

Elie watched as the first groups of people were led away. Behind them in the streets lay all of the things they had not been allowed to take with them: family portraits, suitcases, eating utensils, and other remnants of their once normal lives.

Elie and his family, along with several others, were ordered to march to the second of the two ghettos. Elie cast a backward glance at the home that had been his since birth. In it, he had prayed and fasted and studied. In it, he had felt the love and security of his family. And then, he heard his father weeping.

Elie's mother walked silently in front of him. His seven-year-old sister Tzipora struggled under the weight of her sack. All around them, the police were shouting to the people to run. Old men and women, the sick and the very young, were beaten with clubs as they passed through the streets.

When the people in Elie's group joined those in the second ghetto, they were shocked by what they saw.

Windows smashed, doors ajar, belongings scattered through the streets. Glancing furtively through the open entrance to the home of one of his relatives, Elie could see upturned furniture and books littered on the floor.

Each cattle car held eighty people. One person in each car was put in charge of the others. If anyone tried to escape, the person in charge would be shot. Loaves of bread and buckets of water were delivered to each car. The cars were sealed off and the windows barred. And then, slowly, the train began to move.

Inside the cars, the people stood shoulder to shoulder in the suffocating darkness. Since there was no room to lie down, each took turns sitting down. After days of travel, the water ran out and the people grew ill with thirst. And still the train moved on.

At last the train arrived at its destination: Auschwitz-Birkenau, one of the six extermination camps that the Germans had established.

The doors were opened and the people ordered onto the platform. At the command, each removed wedding rings, watches, and any other gold that they still possessed. At a second command, the men and boys were ordered to march to the left, the women and children to the right.

Elie held onto his father's hand. Searching the crowd for the sight of his mother and sisters, his eyes fell on them, walking with bowed heads in the opposite direction. As they walked, Elie's mother stroked his little sister's long, blonde hair.

The air was stifling and the people choked on the trail of acrid smoke that rose from tall chimneys in the distance. On and on they marched.

The men and boys reached the center of the square. At the front of the line stood the infamous Dr. Mengele with baton in hand, ready for the "first selection." As each prisoner stepped up to be examined, the officer pointed his baton first in one direction and then the other. Those who looked healthy were marched off to the cell blocks. The ill, the elderly, and the lame were sent to the gas chambers.

Elie and his father were among those to survive that first day. His mother and his little sister Tzipora were gassed. On their way to the cell blocks, Elie and his father saw flames shooting up from a ditch. Trucks were unloading the bodies of little children and tossing them into the fires.

Once inside the cell blocks the prisoners were stripped of their clothing except for their shoes. Heads were shaved and all body hair removed. And then the beatings began.

Before sunup the next morning, Elie and the others, still naked but for their shoes, were taken to a second barracks where they were dipped in gasoline for disinfection and then marched into the showers. In still another building, they were issued clothing. A cap, a loose shirt, pants. Next came a second separation, as an SS officer ordered all skilled workers to march.

Elie and his father, along with those in the second group, were taken to another building. More beatings took place, during which Elie saw his father struck to the ground. Then, after another march on the run, the prisoners came to the entrance of a second camp. SS troops surrounded them, brandishing machine guns as police dogs stood at alert by their sides.

As the men and boys passed through another gate, they looked up at a huge sign that read, "Work Is Liberty!" They had arrived at Auschwitz.

Once again, the prisoners were ordered to remove their clothing and were taken into the showers. These were followed by endless hours of standing outside in the open air, clad only in their shoes. Dusk came and the skies grew dark as heavy smoke from the crematoriums billowed above their heads. Finally, at midnight, the prisoners were assigned to a new barracks. Rows of wooden bunks stacked in tiers stretched down a long, dark room where the only light came from skylights high above. Two men were directed to each bunk. There were no mattresses.

On the following day, Elie and the others were given new uniforms. That afternoon, each prisoner stood in line to receive a tattoo on the left arm. With this final humiliation, each had been reduced to a nameless number.

Three weeks later, after a long walk of four hours through the German countryside, the new prisoners arrived at a third concentration camp called Buna.

Here, Elie and the others were given medical examinations, after which their teeth were checked by a line of dentists. On their note pads, the dentists recorded a mark beside the number of each prisoner who had gold crowns or fillings in his mouth. Gold was valuable to the Germans. Elie had one gold crown.

When the examinations had been completed, each of the prisoners was given his work orders. Elie was assigned to an electrical equipment warehouse.

One day while Elie was working in the warehouse, a

guard came toward him and began beating him. Then the guard threw his entire weight on the boy and continued to beat him on his head, face, and body. Elie took each blow in silence, knowing that if he cried out he could be killed.

At last, the beatings stopped and the guard moved away. Elie crawled back to where he had been working. Leaning against the wall for a moment, he closed his eyes as the pain from the beating ran through his body. Soon, he felt a gentle hand wiping the blood from his face. Elie looked up to see a young girl smiling faintly at him. Then, pushing a small crust of bread into his hand, the girl whispered a few comforting words and went quietly back to her work place.

One day, the leader of Elie's labor gang threatened to take out his gold crown. The boy told him that one of the dentists had already noted the crown on the record sheets. If the gang leader stole the crown without the dentists' knowledge, he could get into trouble. The gang leader laughed and made it clear that it would be Elie who would get into trouble if he didn't obey orders.

When Elie's father heard what had happened, he told his son that he must not give in to the gang leader's intimidations. Elie argued that if he refused to respond to the threats, it could be dangerous for both of them.

Several days later, Elie's warning came true when the gang leader discovered that his father could not march in step as the prisoners moved from one place to another in the camp. Each time Elie's father broke the rhythm of the compulsory beat, the gang leader hit him with his club.

Weeks went by, and the clubbings continued. Finally, Elie could stand it no more, and begged his father to let him give in to the bully. The gold crown was removed with a rusty spoon.

As the months passed, the Allies stepped up their bombing raids over Germany. Frequently, Elie and the others heard the distant thumps of antiaircraft guns, and on most nights, squadrons of American and British planes could be seen flying back to their bases in England.

On a Sunday morning late in 1944, when Elie's half of the prisoners were in their barracks and the others were at work in their labor gangs, Buna's air raid sirens sounded. Immediately, all of the guards in the watch towers left their posts and raced for the shelters. SS troops took up their stations throughout the camp to shoot any prisoners who tried to escape during the air raid.

As the sirens continued to wail, a man crept out from one of the buildings and slowly crawled toward two large soup cauldrons that had been set up outside for the noon ration. As yet unnoticed by the guards, the prisoner inched toward the cauldrons. Reaching the first of the two cauldrons, he struggled to lift himself upward toward the opening in the top. Suddenly, the roar of machine guns exploded in the air and the prisoner fell back to the ground. After a brief moment, he lay still.

Soon, the drone of airplanes was heard overhead, and as Elie listened, bombs began to rain down on the camp. Buildings trembled and the skylights in Elie's barracks rattled with the barrage. Buna was under attack. The prisoners shouted to one another. Would the Allies rescue them today?

After an hour, the bombings ceased. Outside, all was quiet. At last, the sirens sounded the all-clear.

As the air raids increased and the Germans continued to be beaten back throughout Europe, Nazi retaliations against the tens of thousands of prisoners at the Buna camp grew more frequent. Hangings became common practice, and at each, the prisoners were forced to witness the final agony. Food rations dwindled and the men and boys grew weak with hunger.

September came, and with it, Rosh Hashanah, the holy day that observed the passing of the Jewish calendar year. On the evening before, all of the prisoners who were able to walk gathered together outside their barracks. The solemn prayers were uttered, first by the officiant, and then by the thousands of men and boys who had crowded into the area. Elie heard the mournful chants as each prayer was offered. With each response came the anguished cries of a desolate people. The voice of the officiant grew faint as he choked on his words. At the end of the service the prisoners uttered the Kaddish — the Hebrew prayer for the dead — in memory of lost parents, wives, children, sisters and brothers and friends.

Elie and his father were separated from each other. Elie was moved to a new barracks and assigned to a new labor gang. For twelve hours each day, he dragged and lifted building blocks heavier than his own small frame. Beside him worked a man who had once been a Rosh-Yeshiva, a teacher of the Hebrew scriptures.

Soon after Elie's arrival, the prisoner spoke to him. Whatever the cost, the young boy must not give in to the evil that surrounded him. He must keep his mind alert in order to preserve his soul. In order to do so, one must study.

Day after day, Elie and the prisoner recited the

scriptures together. As they worked, the pages of the Torah slowly crept into the young boy's mind and the years of study in the little town of Sighet came back to him. Eventually, Elie began to visualize the lines of the sacred scriptures, and felt himself growing stronger once again in spirit. And then one morning, the man was gone.

Elie's block leader, a Jew from Czechoslovakia, came into the barracks before mealtime one evening, announcing that two bowls of soup would be awarded to the prisoner who could tell the best story. Eager for the extra ration, one after another of the inmates responded.

Finally, the block leader came to Elie. After much urging, the young boy began to describe the meal that he had so often pictured in his mind — the Shabbat meal held each Friday in his home in Sighet. The starched white damask, the silver candelabra, his little sister Tzipora setting the special dishes on the table. The sacred songs and the blessing of the bread and wine. And grandfather seated among the others gathered for the meal. All around him, the prisoners listened with heads bowed. Each had shared in Elie's story. Each had broken the bread and sipped the wine. Throughout the barracks, a hushed silence prevailed. That evening, Elie Wiesel was awarded two bowls of soup.

Early one evening after the prisoners had returned from work, they were told not to go into the yards after the food ration had been handed out. A selection was about to take place, and the weakest of the prisoners would be sent to the gas chambers.

Later that night, as the prisoners stood naked by their bunks, three SS officers came into the barracks followed by Dr. Mengele, the Nazi officer who had greeted them all at Birkenau.

According to procedure, each prisoner was to run as fast as he could down the length of the aisle to the place where the officers stood. There, the prisoner's skin was checked for color, the arms and legs tested for strength, the eyes examined for alertness. With notebook in hand, Mengele made a mark here and there beside a prisoner's number. Finally, it was Elie's turn.

With all the strength he could muster, Elie ran down the aisle past the prisoners standing at attention. Would tonight be the night he would be taken? Facing Dr. Mengele, Elie's mind raced as the color of his skin was examined, and then his arms and legs and eyes. At last the order came for him to return to his bunk. He prayed that Mengele had not put the dreaded mark beside his number.

Elie was not chosen for the furnaces that night. But others were . . .

Early one morning while Elie was standing in line waiting for his labor gang to march to the building site, his father came to tell him that the time had finally come. He was one of those who had been selected. With eyes tormented by fear and hunger, Elie's father reached under his shirt and brought out his eating utensils. Someday, Elie could trade them if he had to for a piece of bread.

When the order came for Elie's group to march, he saw his father walk to the wall of a building and lean against it. Suddenly, Elie's father started running toward the group. But it was too late. The group had passed through the gate.

Throughout the day, Elie performed his duties at the building site as though he were in a trance. Knowing of his anguish, several of the workers tried to assure him that his father would be relieved of his sentence.

Returning to the camp later that day, Elie ran to his father's barracks. Moving down the aisle to his father's bunk, he could scarcely believe his eyes. There, on the bunk before him, sat his father! He had convinced the officers that he could still work, and therefore was still useful. Elie and his father held on to each other for a brief moment. And then, reaching into his shirt, he brought out his father's eating utensils and handed them back to him.

With the arrival of winter, the days grew short and the nights bitter with freezing cold. Elie and the other prisoners felt the wind whipping through their shirts as their bare hands struggled with the building stones. Rumors spread that the Germans were losing on all fronts and that the war would soon be over. Elie could not allow himself to think of such a miracle.

And then the word came. Buna was to be liquidated and the prisoners would be taken to another concentration camp called Buchenwald. Those who were ill or too weak to walk would be left behind.

On the night that the news broke, Elie walked through the snow to his father's barracks. Whatever happened now, they must not be separated. Elie wondered if his father were strong enough for the journey. Would he be able to keep up with the others?

Together, the father and son spoke of their concerns

and of the certainty that those who remained in Buna would be exterminated. Most likely the camp itself would be blown up, to destroy all evidence of what had taken place there. In the end, the two decided that they stood a greater chance of survival by marching to Buchenwald.

That night, as Elie lay in his bunk, the skylights above him rattled with the vibrations of distant gunfire. The Russians were advancing.

In the morning, the prisoners were given an extra ration of bread. In the storage rooms, the guards allowed them to take whatever items of clothing they could fit over their uniforms. Blankets would serve as coats.

By nightfall, all was ready. Searchlights blazed through the darkness, illuminating tens of thousands of prisoners as they lined up in formation. Wrapping their blankets tightly about them, they waited silently in the falling snow for the units ahead of them to move. At last, Elie's unit heard the order to march.

Surrounded by SS officers and their dogs, the prisoners marched through the countryside. Wind whipped about them in sudden gusts, and snow bit into their faces. From every direction, the officers shouted at them to move faster and faster until, finally, they were running. Through village after village the prisoners ran until those who could no longer keep up fell behind. Some of them dropped down into the snow and were trampled to death. Despite the confusion, Elie managed to find his father.

Numbness set in, and with it the desire to let oneself go, to give up, and to fall with the others. Because of his father, Elie knew that he must go on. He must take care of his father, running alongside of him, weaker now and short of breath.

On and on through the night the prisoners ran, twenty miles, twenty-five, thirty, and more. It was an endless procession moving in silence as the bodies of the fallen bloodied the snow. Elie felt himself pushed along by the mob. To stop now meant death.

At dawn, the order came to rest. Elie and his father took refuge in an abandoned factory, along with a crowd of other prisoners. Each took turns at sleeping. They had covered more than forty-three miles.

The snow continued throughout the day while the prisoners rested. Elie and his father fought against the hunger and thirst that wracked their bodies. At dusk, they were on the move again, leaving behind the dead, the wounded, and those who could no longer continue.

The march was less ordered now. Beside them, the prisoners heard the roar of motorcycles as SS officers shouted to them to press on. Soon, they would arrive in Gleiwitz.

Passing through the barbed wire, Elie and his father were ordered into a crowded barracks, stumbling over men who had dropped to the floor with exhaustion. For three days, they remained at Gleiwitz, without food or water. As the hours passed, the thud of artillery guns grew closer and closer.

On the final day, the prisoners were given a small ration of bread and ordered into open cattle cars. SS troops moved up and down the train platform with their dogs, shouting orders. The last stage of the journey to Buchenwald had begun.

For ten days, the train pushed through the countryside, past villages and farmlands. The snow continued to fall, covering the prisoners huddled in their blankets. Each morning the train stopped, and those who had died during the night were taken away.

On the evening of the tenth day, the train arrived in Buchenwald. At the beginning of the journey, one hundred prisoners had been crammed into each of the cattle cars. In Elie's car, only twelve had survived.

* * *

The next morning, Elie's father, struck down by hunger and fever, was taken to a barracks with other sick prisoners. Elie brought him something to drink and spoke what words of comfort he could.

Days passed and Elie's father grew weak with dysentery. Prisoners in bunks to either side stole his rations of bread and struck out at him because he could no longer go to the latrines. Desperate and unable to get any help, Elie moved into the barracks and found an empty bunk above his father's. Here, he would be able to watch over him.

One week later, on January 29, 1945, the young boy's father died.

For the next four months Elie moved about, seeing nothing, feeling nothing. He had lost his mother, his little sister, and his father. Of his two older sisters he had had no news. Life was empty of meaning. Transferred to the children's block with six hundred others, he spent the days lying on his bunk, staring into space.

On the eleventh of April, the Americans arrived. Elie and the other children in his barracks listened as the first of the tanks rolled into the camp. The tanks stopped and the soldiers got out. Silence descended as the men walked up and down the yards, unable to believe what they saw — the emaciated prisoners, the creamatoriums, and the open pits where the remains of skeletal bodies lay.

Soldiers came into Elie's barracks, their faces contorted, tears running down their cheeks. As they moved down the rows of bunks, some of the men gave way to sobs of anger and rage.

One day, Elie, like Nechama Bawnik, Karla Poewe, and others, would write of his experiences. In 1986, he was awarded the Nobel Peace Prize.

Today, as a writer, teacher, and lecturer, Elie Wiesel works tirelessly for the cause of human rights throughout the world. Addressing what he considers to be the moral obligation of people everywhere to protect the welfare and rights of others, he writes: "There is so much to be done, there is so much that can be done . . . one person of integrity can make a difference, a difference between life and death."

A Time of Shame

An early morning sun inched its way above the horizon, sending streaks of pink and gold across the tropical sky. At the Pearl Harbor Naval Base in Hawaii, U.S. seamen stationed aboard the dozen or so vessels lining the docks chatted with one another over a quiet Sunday breakfast, read the papers, or enjoyed a leisurely stroll along the decks. Others, in anticipation of a day's leave ashore, took advantage of an extra hour's sleep.

Suddenly, the roar of aircraft shattered the peaceful calm of a new day. Minutes later, waves of Japanese planes thundered across the base, dropping tons of torpedo bombs on battleships and destroyers anchored in the harbor. The attack came swiftly and without warning, allowing no time for defensive action. When it was over, more than three thousand seamen, officers, soldiers and civilians had been killed.

Hundreds were trapped aboard the sinking ships, bodies floated in bloodied waters, and fires raged out of control. In the worst disaster in United States Naval history, eight American battleships, three light cruisers and three destroyers had been lost. The date was December 7, 1941, a day that President Franklin Delano Roosevelt would call "a day that will live in infamy."

Thousands of miles away, seven-year-old Jeanne Wakatsuki stood with her mother and her two sisters-in-law, watching a cluster of fishing boats as they sailed from the San Pedro Harbor at Long Beach, California. It was a family custom that Jeanne loved, and like the others, she kept her eyes fastened on her father's craft, *The Nereid*, watching it shrink to a tiny white dot as it moved into the distance.

Jeanne's father, Ko Wakatsuki, and her two brothers, Bill and Woody, were commercial fishermen who plied the waters north and south along the California coast, following the schools of sardines that would later be sold to the local canneries. Setting out to sea, they would often be gone for weeks, filling their nets with the precious cargo that was their livelihood.

Minutes went by, while Jeanne and the others waited for the fishing boats to slip beneath the horizon. But as they watched, the vessels appeared to have slowed their pace, or to have stopped altogether. And then, from somewhere along the wharf, a young man started running and shouting something about the Japanese bombing of Pearl Harbor.

As the man broadcast his news to clusters of people standing about the marina, the fishing boats turned around and headed back to shore. Onboard *The Nereid,* Ko Wakatsuki and his sons huddled around their ship's radio, listening to the news of the terrible tragedy.

At home later that evening, Jeanne watched her father burn the Japanese flag that he had brought from Hiroshima, Japan, as a seventeen-year-old. In addition to the flag, Ko Wakatsuki destroyed papers that would have revealed his status as an alien, since, like thousands of other Japanese-born people in the United States, he was forbidden by law to apply for citizenship.

Within hours of the Japanese attack, agents of the government and the FBI swept through cities and towns throughout the West Coast. Japanese banks, businesses, stores, and marketplaces were closed and padlocked, and the homes of all first generation Japanese were searched. Radios and cameras were destroyed, along with ceremonial weapons, clothing, and dolls.

Rumors were rampant, and fears of a Japanese invasion on the West Coast spread throughout the country. President Roosevelt addressed the Congress the following day, and later spoke to the nation by radio. America was at war.

The attack on Pearl Harbor revived the resentment the country had felt toward the Japanese since their arrival on United States soil nearly one hundred years earlier. For first generation Japanese, or Issei, as they were known among themselves, life was particularly difficult. Denied citizenship, they could not own land, nor could they vote. Stores, businesses, and markets were either rented or placed in the names of their children, the Nisei, or natural-born citizens of the United States. And since the passing of the Immigration Act in 1924, no Japanese had been allowed to immigrate.

For two long weeks, Jeanne Wakatsuki and her family waited in fear as Japanese aliens were taken into custody on the grounds that they were potential spies. And then one night, while everyone was visiting with Woody and Woody's wife, Chizu, on Terminal Island, near Long Beach, two FBI agents came to arrest Jeanne's father, along with others in the fishing community.

During the days that followed, government agents surrounded the area, destroying short-wave band radios used by wives to keep in contact with their husbands at sea. Ordinary household items such as flashlights and kitchen knives were confiscated as well.

When Jeanne's mother learned that her husband

had been sent into long-term imprisonment at Fort Lincoln, in Bismarck, North Dakota, she moved her family from their big frame house in Orange Park to Terminal Island, feeling safer to be near Woody and Chizu. But two months later, authorities at the Long Beach Naval Base, fearful of having so many Japanese living nearby, ordered the entire area cleared, despite the fact that most of the community's residents were American citizens. Jeanne and her family were given twenty-four hours to leave.

Shortly after, swarms of secondhand dealers descended upon the island, offering bargain prices for furniture, china, and family heirlooms they knew that the Japanese would be forced to sell. One dealer offered Jeanne's mother fifteen dollars for an entire set of bone china. When the woman pleaded for a higher price and the man refused, she broke the dishes, one by one, while the dealer watched in disbelief.

Leaving Terminal Island, Jeanne and the others found living quarters in a minority ghetto in Los Angeles, and the adults took whatever menial work they could find in order to survive. But everyone in the Japanese community felt the tensions of the times and the bitter resentment of Caucasian Americans toward them. The country was now at war with Germany as well as Japan, and young men and women everywhere were joining the armed forces. The war effort was under way and the Japanese were outsiders. Any one of them could be a potential threat to the country, a spy perhaps, or a saboteur.

As hatred of the Japanese community mounted, threats and insults appeared on the windows and doorways of confiscated properties. Cartoons ridiculing the people flooded newspapers and magazines. *Life* printed an article warning Americans about the differences between the physical features of the friendly Chinese and the enemy Japanese. Then came the announcement of President Roosevelt's Executive Order 9066, which gave the War Department authority to establish ten permanent relocation camps in isolated areas of the country to house more than one hundred thousand evacuees. Jeanne Wakatsuki and her family were ordered to report to the Manzanar Camp, in a desolate, uninhabited region north of Los Angeles. With this final blow, the peaceful, protected world of a seven-year-old child was torn apart. Life would never be quite the same again.

Jeanne's father, Ko Wakatsuki, was the eldest son in a distinguished family that for hundreds of years had belonged to the *samurai* class. In the ancient Japanese feudal system, the *samurais* were ranked just below the nobility, and were highly respected for their training as warriors.

By the early part of the century, the Wakatsukis were no longer warriors, but they retained their time-honored social status in the city of Hiroshima. Ko's grandfather had been a judge and magistrate, several aunts were among the first women in Japan to complete a university education, and an uncle had been a general.

Ko attended a military school, bound for a naval career, but by the age of seventeen, was restless for a different kind of life. In 1886, the Japanese government had lifted its ban on emigration, making it possible for people to leave the country to find a new life abroad.

Taking advantage of the opportunity, Ko Wakatsuki, headstrong and looking for adventure, left Hiroshima in 1904, arriving in Honolulu, Hawaii, where a cousin was a schoolteacher. After several weeks, relatives introduced him to an American lawyer who offered him three years' work as a houseboy, a room of his own, and ship's passage to the United States as payment for his services.

At the end of this period, the lawyer and his family returned to their Idaho home, with Ko accompanying them as valet, cook, and chauffeur. Ko stayed with the family for two years, perfecting the English that he had first studied at his school in Japan, and reading everything he could to prepare for life as a student at the University of Idaho, under the generous sponsorship of his patron.

Later, while working in Spokane, Washington, during a summer holiday from his college studies, Ko met Riku Sugai, a beautiful young woman who was the daughter of a local farming family. Within a short time, Ko left college and the two eloped, heading south to Salem, Oregon, where Ko became a cook and Riku found work as a nurse and dietitian.

After the birth of their first child in 1916, Ko and Riku moved to Seattle, Washington, where Ko turned to lumberjacking. Years passed, and Ko, ever eager for the big opportunity that would make his fortune, changed jobs frequently. Babies came, one after another until there were nine.

Eventually, the Wakatsuki family settled in California, where Ko, unable to own property, leased a fruit and vegetable farm. For a time all went well. But just as he was beginning to make a good profit from the business, the Depression hit, and Ko lost the lease on the farm.

For the next several years, the Wakatsukis moved

from place to place along the California coast, finding temporary employment as migrant workers on the farms. Everyone worked, including the children.

By the mid-thirties, times had improved slightly, but Ko had had enough of farming. Turning to fishing, he moved his family to Santa Monica, California, and after years of hard work and long hours at sea, Ko Wakatsuki was able to lease a beach house in Ocean Park, two fishing boats, and a second hand car. Life was improving.

Jeanne Wakatsuki was two years old when her father moved the family to Ocean Park. She was a happy child, full of fun, energy, and imagination. Her favorite place to play was on the merry-go-round at the Ocean Park Pier, where she would ride the splendid stallions and race along through fanciful journeys to magical lands. Jeanne loved the pier, with its shooting galleries, cotton candy, and saltwater taffy. It was her special playground.

In 1940, Jeanne's parents celebrated their twenty-fifth wedding anniversary. It was a beautiful day, with relatives and friends joining the festivities. Ko, elegantly dressed in a new suit, silk tie, and stickpin, stood at the head of the table, surrounded by his wife and children. In front of him was a table crowded with silver gifts and traditional foods like abalone salad, lobster, chicken teriyaki, and little seaweed-wrapped balls of rice called *sushi*. Next to Ko stood Riku, beaming with pride and more beautiful than ever in a long, rose-colored dress. There was much to be thankful for in this land of opportunity.

One year later, America and Japan were at war.

In April of 1942, Jeanne Wakatsuki sat on a duffel bag in front of a Buddhist church in Los Angeles. On the collar of her coat, a government official had pinned a tag bearing the identification number that had been given to the family. Along with her mother, sisters, brothers and in-laws, the little girl waited in the raw mist of an early morning for the bus that would take them north to the internment camp at Manzanar.

When the time came for the departure, each of the evacuees was given a box lunch for the long journey ahead. Jeanne's mother and brothers had been able to convince the authorities that their large family had to stay together. Many people were not so fortunate, and spent anguished months separated from relatives who had been taken to one of the other nine camps.

The exhausted group of internees arrived at Manzanar shortly before sunset, and were shocked by what they saw. Everywhere they looked, groups of anxious people searched for missing relatives, and piles of luggage and sacks of housewares lay strewn on the ground. The camp, situated in the middle of a windswept desert, was completely surrounded by a barbed-wire fence. Along the fence at spaced intervals were heavily armed guards in elevated watch towers. Inside the area, row after row of hastily constructed barracks stood ready to house ten thousand enemy aliens. Jeanne and her family were among them.

Before they could carry their duffel bags and few belongings to their assigned quarters, the people were ordered into the mess hall for dinner. The Wakatsukis joined a long line of evacuees waiting outside for their turn to enter the building. The air was dry and a choking wind coated their clothing with sand. Within minutes, their faces were covered with a powderlike substance that clung to their mouths and stung their eyes.

Finally, it was time to move inside. Camp officials handed Jeanne and the others army mess kits and issued them rations of canned beans, sausage, and rice that was smothered in syrup and canned apricots. Jeanne was sickened by the food, especially the rice which, at home, would never be sweetened and used as a dessert. As she started to protest, Riku quickly silenced her, and the family hurried off to find an empty space on the floor where they could eat their meager supper.

Jeanne and the others were assigned to block 16, a group of barracks that had been crudely put together of pine planking and tarpaper. The buildings stood on concrete blocks raised two feet or so above the desert floor; each one was divided into six tiny family units no larger than a living room. A single light bulb dangled from the ceiling and a small oil stove served as a heater. The Wakatsukis were given two of these units, army cots, blankets, and flimsy mattress covers. Jeanne's brothers were permitted to stuff the covers with straw that had been unloaded outside of the barracks.

Next came the task of dividing the two units for privacy. Bill and Woody Wakatsuki, each of them married and one with a baby, hung blankets between them. Jeanne, her mother, grandmother, and other brothers and sisters crowded themselves into the space that was left.

When Jeanne opened her eyes the following morning, shivering with cold, a layer of desert sand covered the floor. More sand coated the cots, the army blankets, and the clothes that Riku had tucked around each of the children for warmth during the night. Glancing about the area, she could see open spaces between the floorboards and holes where pinewood knots had once been.

While Jeanne's mother lay staring at the dreadful surroundings, Woody took charge of the situation, ordering everyone to get dressed and to help with the cleaning. With his father in prison, Woody, as the eldest son, had become the head of the family.

Later, Woody found several tin can lids and a hammer to nail them over the holes in the floor. Jeanne's older sister, May, worked at sweeping away the sand, fighting to keep up with the winds that forced it back through the cracks in the walls.

"Woody, we can't live like this," Riku said in a voice that was barely above a whisper. *"Animals* live like this!"

Woody wrapped his arms around his tiny mother, smiling to hide his grief. "We'll make it better, Mama. You watch. . . ."

During the months that followed, sixteen more blocks of barracks were added to the already overcrowded camp. Surplus clothing from World War I — coats, and knitted caps, ear muffs and canvas leggings — were shipped in to clothe people unprepared for the bitter winds that swept down from the Sierra mountains.

As time wore on, the disastrous living conditions at Manzanar worsened. Like the facilities at all of the other hurriedly constructed camps, nothing worked. Electric generators frequently broke down, as did the heating and the water supply. Latrines overflowed, forcing people to walk long distances to other sections of the camp. Women raised in cultured surroundings, such as Jeanne's mother, found the conditions intolerable.

Jeanne and all of the younger children at Manzanar were given shots against typhoid infection, but they were constantly ill with stomach cramps and high fevers. In the poorly refrigerated kitchens, food spoiled, and most of the cooks — volunteers from among the internees — had never cooked for large groups of people before.

For the adults, the gradual breakdown in family traditions was painful. Families that had been accustomed to sharing an orderly meal together could no longer do so. Elderly people who could not walk to the mess halls had to eat alone, and teenagers frequently slipped away to look for food in other buildings. In families like the Wakatsukis, heads of households were absent. Living conditions in the barracks were so overcrowded that people returned to them only to sleep at night.

In time, Jeanne's mother found work as a dietitian in the camp and was away for long hours each day. Woody volunteered as a carpenter and Bill was made a roofing foreman. Another brother headed a reservoir crew, guarding the aqueducts that brought the water supply into Manzanar. Jeanne, left on her own much of the time, roamed through the camp on days when her stomach cramps eased.

One day, soon after the family's arrival, the little girl caught sight of a huge pile of books that had been donated by civic organizations, since there were as yet no schools or libraries in the camp. The books, torn and water-soaked after a sudden thunderstorm, had been left at the side of a building since there was nowhere to put them. Jeanne picked up one of them that was lying open on the ground. A picture of a beautiful girl with long, golden hair captivated her. Sitting down amidst the rubble, Jeanne turned the pages slowly and discovered that she could read the words. The story was of Rapunzel. The book was Hans Christian Andersen's *Fairy Tales.* Months had passed since Jeanne had been in a classroom or had a story to read. That afternoon, she read the entire collection of stories, returning to the site for days afterward to devour her newly found treasures.

After an absence of nearly a year, Ko Wakatsuki was released from imprisonment in North Dakota and reunited with his family at Manzanar. Stepping off the bus, he hobbled, weakened and gaunt, on a wooden cane that he had made for himself after his toes had been severely frostbitten. Imprisoned after being accused of supplying Japanese submarines with oil, he was finally released when it became clear that the drums on board *The Nereid* were, in fact, filled with fish bait for his schools of sardines.

Months of interrogation and separation from his family had left Jeanne's father an angry and embittered man. And the sight of his lovely wife and children being forced to live behind barbed wire added to his sorrow. He refused to leave the barracks, and made Riku bring him rice and fruit syrup from the kitchens where she worked. With these, he made a kind of wine, and took to drinking heavily. On his worst nights, he would shout at Riku and threaten to kill her.

In December of 1942, a riot broke out at Manzanar. Frustrated by their imprisonment and angered over disputes involving problems at the camp, a large mob of internees clashed with military police armed with submachine guns. When the mob refused to disperse, the MPs threw tear gas bombs and fired several shots into the air, injuring ten men and killing two others.

Throughout the night, as families kept vigil over their young, bells from all of the mess halls tolled in commemoration of the dead. Military patrol units combed the roadways between the barracks, and searchlights from the watchtowers swept through the camp in eerie silence. Jeanne Wakatsuki did not sleep that night.

After the riot, changes took place at Manzanar. Schools were established, and little rock gardens sprouted in front of many of the barracks. A new camp administrator promised better treatment of the internees.

At about that time, members of the Japanese American Citizens League passed a resolution stating that Nisei interned in the camps were ready to volunteer for active military duty. One month later, in January of 1943, the government responded to the resolution with the announcement that an all-Nisei combat regiment would be established. The Nisei in the camps were relieved and joyful. They were Americans by birth. What better way to prove their loyalty to their country than to volunteer for combat duty?

Unfortunately, this new development caused much dispute between the Nisei and their elders, the Issei, who, because of their Japanese birth, were not permitted to serve in the military. To complicate matters, the government issued a Loyalty Oath, which people of the age of seventeen and older had to sign, either to join the service or to seek sponsored jobs outside of the camps. Many thought that the Loyalty Oath was an insult to the Nisei, while others, like Ko Wakatsuki, felt that they had to sign. If one didn't, he could be sent to Tule Lake, a camp for Japanese American agitators in northern California. Ko strongly opposed allowing Woody to sign, however, fearing that his son would go off to fight for a government that had unjustly placed him behind barbed wire.

Eventually, Woody and his father reached a compromise. He would not volunteer for the fighting unit but would wait to be drafted and take his chances. Other family members found work and sponsors in New Jersey, and were given permits to leave the camp.

By the spring of 1943, thousands of Nisei had left Manzanar and the other camps, and for those who re-

mained, conditions steadily improved. Jeanne and
other family members were moved to Block 28, at the
edge of the camp, and in full view of an old pear orchard, left untouched since the lush, green valley over-
looking the Sierras and Mount Whitney had been
turned into a desert to allow for the flow of mountain
water into the city of Los Angeles.

The move to Block 28 brought about a marked
change for the Wakatsukis. Located near the camp
hospital where Jeanne's mother worked, it was less
crowded, and the living quarters doubled in space.
Jeanne's brothers found sheetrock to line the walls
and ceilings, and linoleum blocks to provide a solid
flooring. With conditions made more bearable,
Jeanne's father's health improved and he drank less.
When camp authorities gave permission for outside
excursions, he would take walks along the dried up
creek beds, searching for driftwood to carve into furniture and lamps for the living quarters. Outside the
barracks, Ko planted a rock garden with stepping
stones leading into the building. Sometimes, he would
paint lovely scenes of the desert, and of Mount Whitney, which brought back boyhood memories of the
majestic Fujiyama of his homeland.

As time passed, other changes took place throughout Manzanar. A group of internees were granted per-

mission to siphon off water from the aqueducts leading into Los Angeles, and a large farm was created outside the camp which eventually produced corn and tomatoes, lettuce, string beans, and other vegetables that provided an ample supply of fresh produce for the mess halls. People took pride in whitewashing their barracks and creating cactus and rock gardens. A group of men who had been professional gardeners before the war designed a small Japanese park complete with waterfalls, ponds, sheltered nooks, and curved wooden bridges. In the evenings, people would stroll along the graveled pathways that looked toward the mountains and, for a brief time, try to forget the barbed wire that enclosed them.

In addition to these improvements, the people established schools and churches in emptied barracks. A new movie theater brought the outside world into reach, and baseball diamonds and judo pavilions were built. For the teenagers in the camp, there were dances on occasion, and one of Jeanne's brothers formed a band to entertain on weekend evenings. Jeanne returned to school and immersed herself in her studies. A glee club was formed with girls from the fourth, fifth, and sixth grades participating. Forty students, Jeanne among them, sang at school assemblies and talent shows.

The War Relocation Authority, eager to ease tensions in the camps, sponsored a recreation program. With leaders hired by the government group, students were permitted to take weekend hikes and go on overnight camping trips. Jeanne looked forward to these outings and the freedom they allowed.

Throughout Manzanar, as in other camps such as Gila in Arizona and Topaz in Utah, classes outside the schoolrooms were organized. Young people and adults alike could participate in literature courses, traditional Japanese arts such as needlework, judo and kendo. Theater groups formed, and acting lessons were taught by people with interest in the creative arts. Jeanne took instruction in baton twirling and later joined a baton club at her school.

In August of 1944, more than two years after Jeanne and her family had been taken to Manzanar, Woody Wakatsuki received his draft notice. The following November, as winds swept through the desert camp and whipped around the corners of the barracks blocks, Jeanne and the others walked with him to the main gate, and watched as he boarded one of the waiting buses. Like those who had gone before him, he would at last have the chance to prove his loyalty to his country and to uphold the family honor.

One month later, on December 18, 1944, the

United States Supreme Court, in settling three landmark cases upholding the rights of all Americans, ruled that loyal citizens could not be held in detention camps against their will. (Of the 110,000 Japanese interned, the majority were natural-born American citizens.) This momentous decision paved the way for the eventual closing of all the ten Japanese American detention camps.

During the months that were to follow, Japanese American soldiers would continue to fight with gallantry in seven major battles throughout northern Italy and France. The combined forces of the 100th Infantry Battalion and the 442nd Combat Regiment would be awarded 18,143 medals for valor, among those, nearly 10,000 Purple Hearts. For their bravery, they suffered 9,486 casualties, the highest percentage of the war. In the South Pacific, an additional 16,000 Nisei fought with intelligence units, translating captured Japanese documents for the U.S. military. In all 30,000 men were involved.

At Manzanar, Poston, Heart Mountain, and other camps, the parents of those killed in action accepted their posthumous medals for bravery. Loyalty and honor had prevailed.

* * *

In October of 1945, Jeanne Wakatsuki and the members of her family who had remained at Manzanar were released. They had been among the first to be taken and among the last to gain their freedom. As they moved through the gates, three and a half years of painful memories went with them, and enough scars to last a lifetime.

For Jeanne Wakatsuki and the 110,000 Japanese Americans, the greatest hardship was the loss of personal freedom, the humiliation of being branded enemies of their country. Many Americans outside the gates of the camps would come to agree. One of those, a teacher who had been assigned to one of the camps by the War Relocation Authority, spoke of her experiences in the classroom with the Nisei children.

"It embarrasses me to teach them the flag salute," she commented. "Is our nation indivisible? Does it stand for justice for all? Those questions come to my mind constantly."

Years would pass before justice would indeed be served. In 1986, President Ronald Reagan signed papers that offered the country's official apology and $20,000 to each of the thousands of Japanese Americans for the executive order that had brought heartache and suffering to so many people. For some of those, the wounds would never heal.

Escape from the Blitz

As the first blast of the ship's horn echoed through the cramped staterooms of the S.S. *Britannic* in July of 1940, young Alistair Horne and hundreds of other British evacuees scrambled up the steps leading to the main deck. Dragging their suitcases behind them, they worked their way toward a spot at the railing to watch a knot of little tugboats guide the vessel toward its berth along the Hudson.

For seven days and nights, the *Britannic* had charted her course through the dangerous seas of the North Atlantic, crossing and recrossing her own path to avoid being torpedoed by Nazi submarines. Throughout the passage, Alistair and the other passengers tried not to think about the threat of enemy attack, but at night, while the darkened ship stole through the rough sea, it was impossible not to.

With mixed feelings of relief and homesickness, fourteen-year-old Alistair watched as the skyline of New York City came into view. Tall, slender buildings stood in majestic clusters, and towering above them all was the great Empire State Building. Out in the harbor, the Statue of Liberty welcomed America's newest group of immigrants to her shores.

For months, the German armies had marched through Holland, Belgium, Luxembourg, and France. Everyone in Britain knew of Hitler's boast that his next major offensive would be England. With the country officially at war with Germany, thousands of British children were being sent abroad to stay in homes throughout the United States and Canada.

As the *Britannic* pulled into its berth, Alistair thought of his departure from England the week before. Leaving his boarding school, he had hurried to Ropley — his family's home outside of London — to catch a final glimpse of the surrounding countryside, and bid farewell to his beloved dogs. Would he ever see them, or his home, again? He thought of that frightening moment back in Euston Station in London, standing with his gas mask and identification tags as his father gave last-minute instructions about being thoughtful, working hard, and writing home regularly.

The boy's eyes roamed through the crowd of Americans waiting for the *Britannic* to dock. Would Mrs. Breese be there to greet him? Would she recognize him? It had been some time since she had last visited Ropley.

Alistair Allan Horne was born on November 9, 1925. The only child of Sir Allan and Lady Auriol Horne, he spent his first few years in the care of a number of nannies and governesses. His mother, a beautiful woman with a brooding nature, traveled extensively, writing for British journals and newspapers, and was away from home most of the time. Alistair's father, an English gentleman who had made his money in India during and after the First World War, spent the week in London, traveling by chauffeured limousine to his country estate for the weekend. Alistair saw little of his father during that time. On Sundays, he would watch from the window of the nursery as the limousine left once again for the city, wishing that his father had come to say goodbye.

Just before Alistair's fifth birthday, his mother was killed in an automobile accident in Belgium. Following her death, the boy's father left for a long safari through Kenya, in East Africa. Alistair's mother's name was never again mentioned in the house.

A lonely boy, shy and chronically sick with asthma, Alistair spent his free moments outside of the nursery roaming about the broad lawns and woodlands surrounding Ropley with his dogs. By the age of seven, he was sent off to Eastacre, a small boarding school near Winchester, where he stayed for several miserable terms, bullied by older boys. Later, he attended Ludgrove, an elite dungeon of a place where many of Britain's most distinguished families were represented. More bullying followed for the next three years, as well as fights with classmates and beatings by the headmaster. After Ludlow came a year in Switzerland, and finally, in September of 1939, a term at Stowe, one week after Hitler had invaded Poland.

Alistair Horne would remember his first day in America for the rest of his life. After moving through a makeshift customs inspection on board ship, he was led down the gangplank and straight into the arms of Julia Breese, who welcomed him with an enormous hug and a warm and engaging smile.

Julia Breese had been a friend of Alistair's family for

many years. On her visits to England she often stayed at Ropley, taking long walks with Alistair and the dogs and showing a genuine interest in the child.

When the threat of war became a reality, Alistair's father, like thousands of parents throughout Britain, was eager to move his son out of the country. The perfect answer was Julia Breese and her family. Alistair would attend school in America, and on holidays would divide his time between Julia's home in South Carolina and her sister Rossy Cutler's in New York City and Garrison, New York.

Whisking Alistair away from the crowded port, Julia Breese took her British charge in hand and headed for the New York World's Fair, where the awestruck fourteen-year-old was treated to amazing displays by countries from around the world, and the sight of hundreds of beautiful young women swimming in precision formation in the great Aquacade, accompanied by a huge orchestra.

For the next several days, Alistair toured New York with Julia, circling the island of Manhattan in a boat, riding to the top of the Empire State Building, and consuming huge ice cream sodas. But despite the wonders of the great American city, he kept thinking about what might be happening at home, and wishing he were back at Ropley with his dogs.

Rossy Cutler was as different from Julia as two sisters could be. Fun-loving, adventurous and outgoing, she was a complete contrast to the shy and gentle Julia, but just as warm-hearted. Greeting Alistair with a cheerful squeeze, she immediately made him feel like one of the family. From the first moment, "Ally" was to be her sixth child, and she treated him as her own.

During the weeks that followed, the fourteen-year-old was introduced to a world that was vastly different from his life of austerity at British schools and a strained relationship with a distant father. In the madcap Cutler family, there was much laughter, teasing, and boisterous activity. But there was also a great deal of warmth and support for one another, and certainly, for Alistair.

Many things in America seemed quite strange. At mealtime, the boy was astounded at the huge quantities of food on the table, having grown used to wartime rationing. Equally mystifying were the kinds of dishes served. The bread looked and tasted like a wad of cotton, and something called *peanut butter* wasn't really butter at all, and stuck to the roof of the mouth in a most dreadful way. And then there were dinners with corn on the cob. In England, farmers threw these to the livestock!

Sometimes, when the noise and confusion of the

large household overwhelmed him, Alistair would steal away to the attic room that he shared with Peter Cutler to listen to news reports on the tiny portable radio Julia Breese had bought for him in New York. The situation in England was growing steadily worse, and the threats from Hitler more ominous. With each new report, the boy's homesickness deepened.

In August, Alistair spent several weeks on Martha's Vineyard with the Cutlers and Julia Breese, in a rented house in Edgartown that quickly filled to the brim with Cutler cousins, friends of the family, and an assortment of guests popping in and out. During this time, Peter Cutler, five years older than Alistair, took his new British friend under his wing, introducing him to sailing aboard a Cape Cod cat-about, and teaching him the difference between a schooner, a ketch, and a yawl. The two boys spent hours combing the harbor and talking to the swordfishermen. Alistair learned to love the barbecues on the beach, with clams and oysters and freshly picked blueberries for dessert before a rowdy game of touch football.

During those weeks on the Vineyard, there were quiet times when Alistair would lie on the beach by himself, watching the waves roll in from the sea and wondering about life on the other side of that seemingly endless stretch of water. The Battle of Britain had begun, and invasion by the Germans seemed certain. Letters from his father, short and irregular, spoke of Churchill's gallant leadership and the Londoners' courage in the face of overwhelming odds. Thinking about it all, the boy wondered if he would ever be able to go home again, or worse, whether England would survive in the end.

In September, Alistair Horne entered Millbrook Academy. One hundred miles north of New York, the school was nestled on top of a hill, surrounded by 500 acres of rolling countryside. Under the leadership of a thirty-three-year-old headmaster by the name of Edward Pulling, it had been in existence for only nine years, but had quickly gained a solid reputation for academic standing.

In addition to Alistair, six other British evacuees arrived at Millbrook. Noting the contrast between their boarding schools in Britain and the informality of life at the academy during their first weeks, they were an outspoken bunch, complaining about the food and their studies and ridiculing the American boys for wearing helmets and masks to play rough games like football. Through it all, Alistair was amazed that he and the other "Bundles from Britain" weren't bloodied and bullied because of their remarks. At Ludgrove, they certainly would have been.

While adjusting to their new life at Millbrook, Alistair and the other boys kept in close touch with the news from home. The Battle of Britain continued to rage as the German Luftwaffe began massive bombings over London and other major cities. On September 7, close to one thousand planes thundered across the skies over England, causing heavy civilian casualties and enormous destruction to houses and other buildings. The Blitz, as it came to be called, would continue without letup for eight and a half terrible months, inflicting countless numbers of deaths and eventually injuring 90,000 people.

As the students listened to Edward R. Murrow and Walter Cronkite broadcasting from London, they were frightened and concerned for the welfare of their families. Alistair worried about his father in London, and anxiously waited for word that he had escaped injury. Many of his father's letters never reached the boy, having gone down in sinking ships.

Ten days after the start of the Blitz, an event occurred that was of particular significance to Alistair and the others. On September 17, tragedy struck in the North Atlantic. German submarines torpedoed an evacuation ship carrying 406 passengers. Of those, 256 people were drowned in stormy seas, and 77 of them were children. Having crossed those waters so recently, Alistair found the news chilling.

Despite their worries, most of the evacuees tried to put on a brave front, feeling the interest and support of their teachers and classmates. Alistair, for one, began to take an interest in his studies, encouraged by the efforts of two wonderful teachers. The first was a retired business executive who had recently come to Millbrook as a math instructor. A man of bouncing good humor and energy, Mr. Tuttle was full of unfamiliar terms such as "will wash, won't wash," meaning "it'll work, it won't work," and "duck soup," or "this is going to be a cinch for you, boys!"

The second teacher was Hank Austin, who taught English and American literature. Young, athletic, and completely at ease with his subject as well as his students, Austin taught while sitting on top of his desk, hands wrapped around long, slender legs. To a boy used to lectures delivered in tones of deadly monotony, Alistair Horne loved the way Hank Austin brought the Puritans of Hawthorne's Salem, the mud of Twain's mighty Mississippi and the West of Jack London into reality. By mid-term, an inspired Alistair Horne was reading Hemingway on his own.

One of the most colorful masters on the Millbrook campus was Frank Trevor, the school's biology teacher, who brought with him a mixed bag of birds, insects, and animals that were the beginnings of the Millbrook Academy Zoo. Trevor had a face and body that bore a strong resemblance to Ichabod Crane, and his world revolved around the biology lab and its assorted collections and experiments.

During his first weeks at the academy, Alistair was surprised by the openness of the American students and their good-natured sense of fun; what was totally lacking was the mocking treachery that he had experienced at his British schools. He was also impressed by the seriousness with which everyone took the progress of events in England. The support was comforting and did much to ease the pain of separation from home.

Another remarkable characteristic of Millbrook was the way in which students helped each other. One of the boys, a junior who was extremely handicapped physically, found constant support and encouragement from classmates who cheered him on in his struggle to lead as normal a life as possible.

Edward Pulling, the remarkable headmaster of Millbrook, brought with him a host of fresh ideas when starting his school. In contrast to British schools, for instance, the students wore no uniform. A jacket and tie, accompanied by neatly brushed hair and clean fingernails at mealtime, were the only requirements. Uppermost in importance was the quality of instruction. Teachers were encouraged to be innovative and creative, and respected for their academic excellence. And the attitude that existed between the faculty and their students was one of friendliness and trust.

"The Boss," as Pulling was affectionately dubbed by his students, rewarded the boys for their effort in the classroom. A weekend's leave from school was an envied prize, and those who lacked the ability to excel were given "effort marks," which proved their willingness to try hard. Seniors at Millbrook had the privilege of disciplining students in the lower grades, by "sentencing" them to "The Jug" on Saturday evenings while the rest of the school enjoyed a movie. There, in a room directly beneath the theater, offenders would copy page after page from the *Encyclopedia Britannica* while agonizing over the sounds of the entertainment going on above them.

As the weeks passed, Alistair and his classmates listened to the evening radio broadcasts from London, distressed by the devastation from the relentless bombings by the Germans. One of his father's letters described the disappearance of a favorite pub. Reading the report, the boy realized that the building was less than twenty yards from his father's quarters. After watching a newsreel of St. Paul's Cathedral enveloped in flames, Alistair had nightmares that were so frightening he couldn't watch a school bonfire without becoming sick to his stomach.

As spring came to the rolling hills surrounding the academy and students started training for the season's sports matches, the war in England and Europe had turned for the worse. Alistair and the other British students felt guilty about their life of safety in America. Severely depressed and feeling restless despite the support from teachers and classmates, Alistair wanted to go home. With each new report he grew increasingly anxious. The war in the Atlantic was costing the lives of countless British seamen, and in London, people were going hungry from lack of food. Those letters that did reach the boy reported the deaths of tens of thousands, including relatives in London.

With the close of school for the summer holiday, Alistair spent time with Julia Breese in South Carolina, and the two later joined the rest of the Cutlers for a return to Martha's Vineyard. In the seaside village of Vineyard Haven, Alistair and Peter Cutler, now the closest of friends, waited on tables at a local restaurant, earning seventy-five cents per night and all the lobster and lemon meringue pie that they could eat. But the contrast between the peacefulness of the Vineyard and the sufferings of his people at home were, at times, overwhelmingly painful.

Returning to Millbrook in the fall of 1941, Alistair plunged into his studies. Three months later, America found itself at war with Germany and Japan. President Roosevelt told Winston Churchill that the two countries were "in the same boat now." Despite Roosevelt's comforting words, however, British students at the academy were fearful that the Americans, by their entrance into the war, would cut back their support for organizations such as the British War Relief and the new Lend Lease Program. That was not to be, of course, and young American servicemen and women would soon be heading for British shores to join in the fight against Germany.

As the United States mobilized for war on two fronts, changes were taking place on the school campus. Many of the academy's employees were leaving to join the service or work in defense plants. Wherever possible, Edward Pulling replaced these people with Millbrook students, determined that they would share in the responsibilities of running the school. The boys waited on tables in the dining room, worked in the kitchen, and were trained to perform many duties that had been carried out by academy employees. To save electricity, the school went on daylight-saving time, causing some havoc in the darkened hallways and showers at six o'clock in the morning. Classes in Morse Code and seamanship were conducted. An observer station was set up to spot German bombers in the event of an attack on New York City, and first-aid courses were given by the school nurse.

The months sped by and weekly news reels and articles in *Life* magazine carried vivid photographs of the war in Britain, Europe, and the Pacific. Alistair longed for the day when, as a Millbrook graduate of seventeen and a half, he could enlist for training in the Royal Air Force. Would that day ever arrive?

For several weeks during the summer of 1942, Alistair and a number of other students worked on the school farm, replacing employees who had gone off to war. Working in the fields from dawn until the late hours of the afternoon, they would return, exhausted but browned by the summer's sun. Alistair loved every minute of it, digging into the soil with an energy and strength that he didn't know he had.

After his stint on the farm, Alistair joined the Cutler family on the Vineyard for a brief holiday by the sea before going back to his studies at Millbrook. It would be the last of his summer visits to the island until after the war.

During his final year at Millbrook, Alistair Horne experienced a happiness and sense of fulfillment that he would remember for years to come. He had matured, made many friends, and become a foster member of a family he had grown to love and to admire. Life at the academy had given him a self-confidence that he had never known. Added to this new sense of belonging was the growing knowledge that the tide was gradually turning in the war against Germany.

As a senior, Alistair took on his school responsibilities with gusto, working for the campus newspaper, joining in on class debates on the fast-changing developments in Europe, and entering into a lifetime friendship with his roommate, Bill Buckley, who, in later years, would become the distinguished editor, writer, and news panelist William F. Buckley Jr. He had also become an enthusiastic hockey competitor.

Throughout the year, veterans of British and American campaigns in Europe would come to Millbrook to lecture the students. An officer from a British minesweeper told of exploits in the Atlantic, an American medical corpsman spoke of his experiences in France, and an RAF officer caught Alistair's attention with stories of bombing sorties over Germany.

In the classroom, the sixteen-year-old pored over *Hamlet* and *Ethan Frome* during the day, and at night filled his huge war map with pins indicating Allied successes in Europe. And with the entire student body and faculty of Millbrook, he mourned the death of the beloved Hank Austin, killed in a military air crash.

As graduation time approached, Alistair held on to his dream of joining the Royal Air Force. Although Harvard University had offered him a full scholarship, he turned it down, feeling that his country needed him. Later, if all went well, he would go to on to Cambridge University.

Shortly before Commencement Day arrived (the term — meaning "a beginning" — both baffled and amused him, as so many American words did), Alistair was saddened to receive a chilly note from his father, saying that he was sorry to miss the ceremonies but was unable to get a permit to leave England. At the end, his father added that he didn't really want to make the trip. It would be too expensive.

There were, however, others who would be there to celebrate the big day with Alistair. Julia Breese arrived, along with carloads of Cutlers, to attend the ceremonies and the festivities that followed. In the midst of all the noisy merriment, the seventeen-year-old, now six feet tall, felt the outpouring of warmth and love that he had experienced with this remarkable family since his first days in America.

In the weeks that followed, the days and evenings were filled with farewell parties and twilight barbecues, with reminiscences of good old Millbrook times, and midnight games around the Buckley swimming pool before a final visit with the Cutler clan.

Suddenly, it all came to an end. With mixed feelings of joy and sadness, Alistair knew that it was time to bid good-bye to America and all that he had grown to love and admire. He was going home.

The Silent Rescuer

One thousand years ago, Vikings in their dragonlike longboats sailed out of the northern seas to attack and plunder lands along the western coast of Europe, moving south into the Mediterranean and finally westward across the sea to Iceland, Greenland, and Newfoundland. At various points along the northwestern coast of France, they navigated through rivers that led inland from the sea with such force that the King of France gave in to their might and offered them an area of land that had been so violently sacked he considered it no longer valuable.

The Vikings accepted the proposal, settled in, and conferred upon their chieftain the title of Duke of the Norsemen. Later, the area became known as Normandy.

The province of Normandy is one of the most beautiful in France. The lush countryside is dense with forests and hedgerows, and the rich soil produces some of the finest fruits and vegetables in the country. Along the coastline facing the English Channel, cattle and sheep graze in the marshlands. In the offshore waters, fishermen cast their nets for delicate sole, or move on into the North Sea for an abundance of herring and cod.

The people of Normandy are a rugged and sturdy lot, proud of the land that produced their noble ancestor, William, the Duke of Normandy, Conqueror of all of Britain.

By October of 1940, the province of Normandy was occupied by the Germans. And in a little coastal village near Caen, the people practiced a quiet resistance, casting their eyes upward whenever they passed a group of German soldiers. One of those who followed this custom was a young schoolboy named Pierre Labiche.

The three hundred inhabitants of Pierre's village were aware of the fact that their location near the coast was of great value of the Germans. A network of railways, rivers, and canals would soon turn the region into a strategic center for the mobilization of troops and military supplies. Now, with the Occupation, the once jovial people of the little village were solemn and filled with contempt for their invaders.

One morning, as German troops on motorcycles

roared down the streets of the village, Henri Duplay, the beloved old schoolmaster who had guided the area's children for more than forty years, trudged along the narrow passageway that led to his school. Badly in need of repair, the building leaned up against an ancient church which, like the schoolhouse, had been heavily damaged by air raids.

Along the route, Monsieur Duplay's friend Renaud, the druggist, called a grave *Bon jour* to him. Paul Marcellin, the local butcher, took down his shutters, shrugging over the futility of keeping open a shop that had nothing to sell. Outside the bakery further down the street, a long queue awaited the possibility that a loaf of bread might serve to expand the meager offering of the evening's meal. As in all the other occupied countries, food was controlled by the Germans and was in short supply.

On that particular morning, Monsieur Duplay was weary from lack of sleep. As he walked, he wondered if it would not be wise to give up his work at the schoolhouse and join the Free French and their leader, General Charles DeGaulle, in London. The French Underground Resistance was growing stronger each day and there was so much to be done.

But what would become of his classes if he left? The

school's only other teacher, Mlle. Martin, was tired and overworked as it was. And then, of course, there were his compatriots in the Resistance who needed his advice and who relied upon his judgment.

Reaching the school, Monsieur Duplay climbed the steps and plodded down the hallway to his classroom.

"Bon jour, Maître," the children called out in respectful unison.

"Bon jour, mes enfants," the old schoolmaster replied warmly.

Later that day, as the children tumbled out of the schoolhouse and charged through the iron gate that led to the street, Pierre Labiche followed silently behind the rest. He preferred to walk alone in order to avoid the taunts of four of his classmates. The leader of the group, Jacques Fournier, had earned a reputation as the bully of the school ground, and although Pierre had no fear of the boy he wisely kept his distance.

A mute from birth, Pierre Labiche could neither speak nor hear. Despite these handicaps, however, the child was able to communicate remarkably, having developed a sign language of his own that enabled him to continue his studies and to "speak" to his friends and teachers. Pierre had other attributes as well. With his keen mind and ready smile, he was known and loved by everyone in the village.

Pierre's mother had died when he was an infant and his father, a reservist, had recently been killed fighting the Germans. For some time the boy had lived with his Aunt Paulette in a tiny thatch roofed cottage just outside of the village and facing the sea. To the rear of the half timbered building was an old apple orchard and a small vegetable garden. A densely wooded area lay beyond.

As Pierre made his way down the street, the four boys ahead of him turned around and shouted one last insult. With that, Monsieur Renaud appeared at the doorway of his pharmacy to witness the daily ridiculing. Shaking his head, he called to Pierre and motioned to him to come into the shop. The two shook hands and the boy flashed his familiar smile as he accepted a small package of peppermint tea for Aunt Paulette. Then, from behind the counter, the druggist scribbled a message on a scrap of paper and showed it to Pierre, who silently read the words to himself, *Tonight at 1:30*. The boy acknowledged the message and watched as Monsieur Renaud set fire to the paper with his lighted cigarette. In the next minute, Pierre was gone.

When Pierre arrived at his cottage, he found Aunt Paulette working in her vegetable garden. Although the German Command had ordered her to turn over all the food that she raised, she managed to smuggle much of it to her neighbors and to keep enough for Pierre and herself.

"What the eye doesn't see . . ." Paulette would say to friends who were well aware of her hatred of the enemy. The old woman had lost all the men in her family to the Germans in three wars, the Franco-Prussian War, World War I, and World War II, two of those wars in her own lifetime.

Pierre communicated Monsieur Renaud's message to his aunt, whose hands quickly signed a warning: "Be careful, Pierre, you are now the only man in our family, and we must live on for France!"

That night, Pierre knelt by his bedroom window, staring out through the darkness that enveloped the village each night after the curfew had sounded. Not a light could be seen anywhere. Pierre's eyes searched the cloud-covered skies for aircraft. Lacking hearing, the boy had developed an extraordinary ability to see things others could not.

As his aunt came into the room to bid him goodnight, Pierre suddenly saw the flash of German anti-aircraft fire. In an instant, the sky was flooded with searchlights and Aunt Paulette signaled to him that she could hear a plane approaching.

A minute later, Pierre thought he saw something white floating downward from the sky. Could it be a parachute? The boy's mind raced as he quickly threw on his clothes and gestured to his aunt. Despite the curfew, he was going to find out if he had been right about what he thought he had seen.

In the silence of the woods behind Pierre's cottage, an American airman flying with the RAF released himself from his parachute and folded it quickly as he looked around for a place to bury it. Then, from somewhere close by, he heard something. Turning in the direction of the sound, the airman waited in guarded silence. Seconds passed as he reached for his revolver and switched on his pocket flash. Aiming it cautiously at the ground immediately in front of him, he spotted Pierre a few feet away. As the officer moved toward him, the boy put his finger to his lips to warn him not to speak.

Ripping a knife from his jacket, Pierre motioned toward the airman's parachute and crept to a spot where it could be buried. Then, slashing the material into several pieces, he dug a shallow hole, filled it with the shreds and covered them with tree branches. As Pierre was doing so, the airman whispered to him asking who he was. The boy responded with a smile, grabbing his hand and leading him silently through the woods toward a neighbor's farm.

The two emerged from the trees, and Pierre dropped into a ditch behind the farmhouse, pulling the officer down with him. As the airman lay beside the boy, he heard bombs exploding in the distance. The RAF was doing its work tonight, he thought to himself.

Glancing at the child beside him in the ditch, the officer wondered if he were right in following him. With no time to waste, he decided to take his chances.

After a few minutes, the boy motioned to the airman to crawl along beside him as he dodged between trees and behind hedgerows that led to his cottage.

Once again, Pierre came to a stop, signaling to the officer to lie down. In the distance, he had spotted a faint light moving slowly through the blackness. A second later, the airman heard a car approaching. Suddenly, a searchlight shot through the area and the two hid their faces as the beam from the car swept over their heads.

The car inched closer and then came to a stop a few yards away. Two German officers stepped out of the car. As they stood talking, the pilot listened to their voices, understanding enough of the language to pick up their conversation.

One of the officers said he doubted that anyone could have survived the impact of the explosion on the plane that was hit. And if so, the pilot would have landed closer to the city of Caen.

The second officer was restless and wanted to get back into the protection of the car. These Frenchmen in the Resistance would stop at nothing to stab a German. And besides, he'd had enough of riding around and was ready for a decent glass of Calvados.

As the Germans drove off, the airman glanced at the boy once again. His hunch had been right. The child was trying to protect him.

Silence returned, and the two resumed their journey, crawling through the thick brush of the hedgerows. After a short distance, Pierre halted and pointed to the luminous dial on the pilot's wristwatch, holding up two fingers and nodding his head. Then he crept away. Seconds later, the officer heard the sound of pebbles striking a window glass.

Flight Officer Tracy found himself standing in a woodshed behind Aunt Paulette's cottage. Having introduced himself as an American who had volunteered for the RAF, he acknowledged that he could speak some French and could understand the language quite well. Then he asked about the unusual child who had rescued him.

He was her nephew, the old woman answered, explaining that they communicated with one another through sign language because the boy was mute.

The officer, concerned about his former doubts about the child, apologized. But, he said, wasn't Pierre too young to take such risks?

Aunt Paulette's answer was simple. One was never too old nor too young to fight for his country's freedom.

Moving quickly about the shed, the woman reached into a box and withdrew a shabby old suit. Handing it to the officer, she asked that he put it on and then give her his uniform. At first, the man protested. Did these people know what danger they were in? If the Germans found out . . .

After Tracy had changed into the suit, Aunt Paulette knelt on the floor of the woodshed and began removing a number of heavy logs. Then she pushed aside a dirt covering and removed several wooden planks to reveal an opening in the ground. A number of steps led to a small underground hiding place just large enough for a cot.

Again, the officer argued with the woman. It would be better for all of them if he left.

But Aunt Paulette would have none of it. Lieutenant Tracy was not the first airman she had hidden and he would not be the last. Trust in God and the Resistance, she whispered. Then, handing the airman a bottle of Calvados and a glass, she climbed the steps to the woodshed and whispered, *Bon nuit.*

In class the next morning, Pierre was filled with fear. The *Maître* had not yet appeared, and the students around him were restless. Pierre could think of only one thing. The Germans had learned of the old schoolmaster's activities in the Resistance and had come for him during the night. Pierre clung to the one positive thought in his mind: When he stopped at the druggist's for the morning's messages, nothing had been said about the *Maître*.

At last, Monsieur Duplay appeared. As Pierre breathed a sigh of relief, the schoolmaster explained that he had had a restless night and had overslept. Pierre smiled to himself, knowing the truth about his teacher's secret work.

Monsieur Duplay turned to the blackboard and wrote the name of one of France's greatest heroines, Charlotte Corday, who had been guillotined for her part in the French Revolution. Underneath the woman's name he wrote, "She teaches us how to die." Then, turning back to the students, he began the morning's discussion.

Suddenly, the classroom door burst open and in walked three German officers. One of the officers spoke. Reading the message on the blackboard aloud, he turned on Monsieur Duplay in a rage. What was the meaning of this trash?

This was an important name in France's history, explained the schoolmaster.

France no longer had a history, the officer shot back. The Germans would see to that. Then, turning to face the class, the officer addressed the students.

During the night, German antiaircraft fire had hit an RAF plane, one of a squadron that was returning to its base in England after a raid. A single parachute had been spotted and the airman was believed to be hiding somewhere in the village. A reward of fifty thousand francs would be given to the student who could volunteer information that would lead to the capture of the pilot.

For a time, none of the children spoke. The German

officer was furious, and threatened reprisals if someone didn't speak. Certain facts had surfaced. Among them was a report that a boy had been seen going into the woods near Madame Paulette's cottage.

Finally, Jacques Fournier spoke from the back of the room. The boy whom the authorities were looking for must have been Pierre Labiche.

The students in the classroom were stunned. How could Jacques do such a thing to Pierre?

Ignoring his classmates, Jacques continued. On his way to school that morning, he had seen Pierre eating some chocolate. It must have been English chocolate, because no one in the village had seen that kind of delicacy since before the occupation, Jacques said, pointing to the mute.

The officer walked over to where Pierre was sitting and asked him his name. Sensing that something was terribly wrong, Pierre looked first at the officer and then at Monsieur Duplay.

Getting no response, the German asked the question a second time, and again there was silence. Infuriated, the officer struck Pierre across the face with his leather glove. In spite of the pain of the blow, the child didn't flinch.

Monsieur Duplay spoke. The child was a —

"Quiet!" the German ordered, turning on Pierre for the last time with his question. When Pierre couldn't respond, the officer struck him again with his glove.

As the children watched in horrified silence, Gabrielle, the druggist's daughter, blurted out the fact that Pierre was a mute and could neither speak nor hear.

The officer demanded to know how the schoolmaster communicated with the boy.

By sign language, Monsieur Duplay answered.

Then find out where he was last night, the German said.

The schoolmaster flashed a warning to Pierre. Then he signaled to the boy to go to the blackboard and write that he had been at home with his aunt all evening and that the teacher had given him the chocolate the day before.

While Pierre was writing on the blackboard, Monsieur Duplay opened a drawer in his desk and took out an old wrapper of chocolate, reminding the officer that the Germans had given candy to the schoolchildren on the day they had moved into the village.

With this the officers gave up in frustration, and after a final threat to the students and the schoolmaster, they stormed out of the classroom.

Monsieur Duplay turned to Jacques Fournier, and

in a low voice asked him why he had pointed his finger at Pierre.

As his classmates glared at him, Jacques responded by saying that Pierre wouldn't share his last piece of chocolate with him that morning.

After school that day, Monsieur Duplay asked Pierre if he had anything to tell him.

Yes, the child answered in sign language. Aunt Paulette loved it when visitors came to the cottage.

Nodding his head in understanding, the schoolmaster warned Pierre to be careful. The Germans weren't entirely convinced of his innocence and would be watching for any careless slip-up. And then, as Pierre bid his schoolmaster good day, Monsieur Duplay suggested that he would stop by that evening to write a "letter" for his aunt Paulette.

That evening at Madame Paulette's cottage, Monsieur Duplay memorized Flight Officer Tracy's identification card, going over the information repeatedly so that he could pass it along to the members of his resistance group. That accomplished, he sat down at the kitchen table and wrote a letter which appeared to be meant for Madame Paulette's granddaughter in Alsace but was actually a coded message that Pierre would deliver to the Resistance at the appropriate moment.

As the schoolmaster finished the letter, the sounds of motorcycles roared to a stop outside the cottage. Aunt Paulette ran to the cupboard and brought out an old puzzle for Pierre, handing it to him as a rifle butt banged on the door. Opening it, she stood back as two Germans, an officer and a sergeant, brushed past her.

Pierre busied himself silently with the puzzle, ignoring the Germans as the officer fired question after question at Aunt Paulette. What was her given name?

Madame Labiche.

Who was the boy?

Pierre.

Who was the man?

A friend who was writing a letter for her because she was an uneducated woman and could not write.

What was in the letter, the officer demanded as he snatched the paper from the schoolmaster.

A letter to her only granddaughter, Aunt Paulette responded, telling her that the Germans in the village were treating the people with courtesy and had caused no harm to the citizens. The rest of the letter was filled with chatty news about affairs in the village, she said.

Satisfied with the innocence of the letter, the German moved on to inspect the cottage, leaving the sergeant to guard Pierre and Monsieur Duplay.

Moving about the cottage, the officer resumed his questioning of Madame Paulette.

Noting the three small bedrooms, he went to several of the windows and looked out at the deep hedgerows and the secluded woods beyond the cottage. Suddenly, he caught sight of the shed next to the vegetable garden.

What was in there? the German demanded.

Just an old woodshed, Paulette replied, adding that he was welcome to go in if he didn't mind rats scurrying about his feet.

Turning from the window facing the woodshed, the officer announced that he would be leaving the sergeant at the cottage for a few days, since there was an extra bedroom. Madame Paulette gave her customary shrug and walked back into the kitchen.

Several evenings later, Monsieur Duplay, Monsieur Renaud, and a number of other men and women gathered at the village inn for their weekly choir rehearsal, the single activity allowed by the Germans. As the practice began, Pierre served Calvados to the two officers who sat at a table watching over the proceedings.

At the end of the rehearsal, everyone sat down at a table for a round of Calvados before the curfew sounded. Pierre approached the table with his tray of brandy glasses. As he passed the officers, one of them stuck out his boot and tripped the child, sending him to the floor with the tray.

Monsieur Renaud rushed to pick up Pierre and to help him with the tray and the shattered glasses as the owner of the inn began yelling at the boy. Then, facing the schoolmaster, the owner told him to order Pierre to take the music and the practice accordion to the attic and put them in their usual place.

Quickly, Monsieur Duplay signaled the orders to Pierre, who picked up the music and the instrument. Running up the steps to the attic, he dropped everything in a corner and raced to the trap door in the roof of the attic. Tapping it softly, he opened the door, took Monsieur Duplay's folded "letter" to Aunt Paulette's granddaughter from his mouth and shoved it into a basket that was then lowered from the roof by two members of the French underground.

Closing the trap door, Pierre returned to the room downstairs and continued his cleanup of the brandy and the glasses. While he was doing so, the story of

Flight Officer Tracy was being transmitted by wireless radio to British headquarters in London.

Several days later in class, Gabrielle pushed a coded note into Pierre's hand. Opening it, the boy read the words telling him that his aunt's "medicine" was ready.

That afternoon after school, Pierre stopped at Monsieur Renaud's shop. There, he picked up a bottle containing two capsules and a slip of paper giving directions for taking the medicine at eleven o'clock that night. The boy read the message and handed it back to the druggist, who immediately set it ablaze with his cigarette.

At eleven o'clock that evening at the cottage, Pierre worked on his puzzle while his aunt did her mending and the sergeant wrote to his family in Germany.

Finishing her sewing, Aunt Paulette packed her sewing away, bade goodnight to Pierre and the sergeant, and left the room. With this, the boy took his puzzle to the German and then went to a cask near the kitchen cupboard. There, he poured a large mug of cider and a small one for himself. During the time that the German had been billeted at the cottage, he had grown to like the strange little boy and had taken up the practice of helping him with his puzzle.

While they sat poring over the game, the sergeant quickly emptied his mug of cider, commenting on its fine taste. At Pierre's invitation, the German had another serving.

Before long, the sergeant began having difficulty piecing the puzzle together. Watching him closely, Pierre continued working on the puzzle, pretending not to notice the German as his eyelids began drooping and his body slumped. Minutes later, the man lost consciousness and fell across the table. Aunt Paulette's prescription for the "two capsules at eleven o'clock" had performed their duty.

After checking to make certain that the sergeant was asleep, Madame Paulette hurried to the woodshed to tell Flight Officer Tracy that members of the Resistance would appear shortly to assist him in his escape.

Smiling appreciatively, the airman thanked the old woman for all that she had done and asked to see Pierre before he left. Paulette shook her head, explaining that the child had to keep watch over the German in the kitchen.

With this, the American took off his wristwatch and handed it to the woman, asking her to give the watch to Pierre in gratitude for saving his life.

For a second time, Paulette refused the man's request, saying that it would be dangerous to keep anything that would provide evidence of his having been hidden at the cottage. In the future, there would be others to rescue and more work to be done.

Minutes later, two men dressed in black fishermen's clothing rapped their signal on the door of the woodshed. Madame Paulette whispered her blessing to the officer, and together the three men slipped into the night.

One morning less than a week after Flight Officer Tracy had left, Monsieur Duplay greeted his class and began the morning's lessons. Glancing up from his book, he spotted the raised hand of Gabrielle Renaud, the druggist's daughter. Her father had a question for the schoolmaster, she said. Could Monsieur Duplay explain the words *"the future, the future, the future belongs to me,"* and whether that might have come from a poem?

The old schoolmaster put down his book, and after a brief sigh, responded by saying that the line had indeed been taken from a poem about Napoleon that the great French writer Victor Hugo had written many years before. With that, he signaled the message to Pierre.

Suddenly, a broad grin lit up the boy's face as he recognized the coded message. Flight Officer Tracy had arrived in England. Another Allied pilot had been saved.

Bibliography

Bailey, Anthony. *America Lost and Found*. New York: Random House, 1993.

Berg, Mary. *Warsaw Ghetto: A Diary*. New York: L.B. Fisher, 1945.

Bles, Mark. *Child at War: The True Story of a Belgian Resistance Fighter*. New York: Mercury House, 1991.

Brown, Robert McAfee. *Elie Wiesel, Messenger to all Humanity*. Notre Dame, Indiana: University of Notre Dame Press, 1983.

Carlisle, Olga Andreyev. *Island in Time: A Memoir of Childhood*. New York: Holt, Rinehart, 1980.

Cowan, Lore. *Children of the Resistance: The Young Ones Who Defied the War*. London: Freewin, 1968.

Dwark, D. *Children With a Star: Jewish Youth in Nazi Europe*. Connecticut: Yale University Press, 1993.

Eisenberg, Azreil. *The Lost Generation: Children of the Holocaust*. New York: Pilgrim Press, 1982.

Enser, A.G.S. *Subject Bibliography of the Second World War*. New York: Oxford University Press, 1992.

Estess, Ted L. *Elie Wiesel*. New York: Frederic Ungar Publishing, 1994.

Friedman, Philip. *Their Brothers' Keepers*. New York: The Holocaust Library, 1978.

Gollomb, Joseph and Alice Taylor. *Young Heroes of the War*. New York: The Vanguard Press, 1943.

Hallie, Philip. *Lest Innocent Blood Be Shed*. New York: Harper and Row, 1979.

Horne, Alistair. *A Bundle From Britain*. New York: St. Martin's Press, 1994.

Houston, James D. and Jeanne Wakatsuki Houston. *Farewell to Manzanar*. New York: Bantam Books, 1974.

Hutchinson, R. *How We Lived Then: A History of Everyday Life During the Second World War*. London: Viking Penguin, 1971.

Irons, Peter. *Justice at War*. New York: Oxford University, 1983.

Jackson, Carlton. *Who Will Take Our Children?* London: Methuen, 1985.

Kent, F. *Green Avalanche: The Story of an English Girl's Adventures as a Combatant During World War II*. London: Phthagorean, 1960.

Kitagawa, Daisuki. *Issei and Nisei: The Internment Years*. New York: Seabury Press, 1967.

Meltzer, Milton. *Never to Forget*. New York: Harper and Row, 1976.

Miller, Russell. *Resistance*. New York: Time-Life Books, 1979.

Patterson, Charles. *Anti-Semitism: The Road to the Holocaust and Beyond*. New York: Walker and Company, 1982.

Poewe, Karla Olga. *Childhood in Germany During World War II: The Story of a Little Girl*. Ontario, Canada: The Edwin Mellen Press, 1988.

Rittner, Carol, and Sondra Meyer, eds. *The Courage to Care*. New York: University Press, 1986.

Stadtler, Bea. *The Holocaust: A History of Courage and Resistance*. New York: Behrman House, 1975.

Tatieshi, John. *And Justice for All: An Oral History of the Japanese American Detention Camps.* New York: Random House, 1984.

Tec, Nechama. *Dry Tears: The Story of a Lost Childhood.* New York: Oxford University Press, 1984.

——, *When Light Pierced the Darkness.* New York: Oxford University Press, 1987.

Weinstein, Frida. *A Hidden Childhood.* New York: Hill and Young, 1985.

Westall, Robert. *Children of the Blitz.* London: Macmillan Children's Books, 1995.

Wicks, Ben. *No Time to Say Goodbye: The Story of British Child Evacuees.* New York: St. Martin's Press, 1988.

Wiesel, Elie. *From the Kingdom of Memory.* New York: Simon and Schuster, 1990.

——, *Night.* New York: Bantam Books, 1982.

——, *One Generation After.* New York: Random House, 1965.

Papers, Pamphlets, and Related Articles

Anti-Defamation League, "Human Relations Materials for the School," 1989.

Berenbaum, Michael, Eva Fogelman, Philip Hallie, Marion Pritchard, and Harold M. Schulweis, "Moral Courage During the Holocaust," *Dimensions* 5, no. 3 (1992): pp. 1–16.

Brahman, Randolph L., Norman Cousins, Richard J. Evans, and Deborah E. Lipstadt, "Resisting History: How They Explain (Away) the Holocaust," *Dimensions* 6, no. 1 (1992): pp. 4–24.

Sonnensheim, Frances, Ed.D., "A Short History of Anti-Semitism," The Jewish Foundation for Christian Rescuers/Anti-Defamation League, 1990.

The author gratefully acknowledges the permissions granted and courtesies extended for the use of background material from the following:

Bawnik, Nechama (Tec.). *Dry Tears: The Story of a Lost Childhood*. New York: Oxford University Press, 1984, for the Nechama Bawnik story.

Cowan, Lore. *Children of the Resistance: The Young Ones Who Defied the Nazi Terror*. London: Frewin, 1968, for the Pierre Labiche story.

Gollomb, Joseph and Alice Taylor. *Young Heroes of the War*. New York: The Vanguard Press, 1943, for the Peter Brouet story.

Horne, Alistair. *A Bundle from Britain*. New York: St. Martin's Press, 1993.

Poewe, Karla. *Children in Germany During World War II*. Queenston, Ontario: The Edwin Mellen Press, 1988.

Wakatsuki, Jeanne. *Farewell to Manzanar*. San Francisco: San Francisco Book Company, and Boston: Houghton Mifflin, 1973, and New York: Bantam Books, 1974.

Westall, Robert. *Children of the Blitz*. London: Macmillan, 1995, for the Bessie Shea Story.

Wiesel, Elie. *Night*. New York: Farrar, Straus and Giroux, 1982; original French edition published by Les Editions de Minuit, Paris, 1958.

Every effort has been made to trace copyright holders.

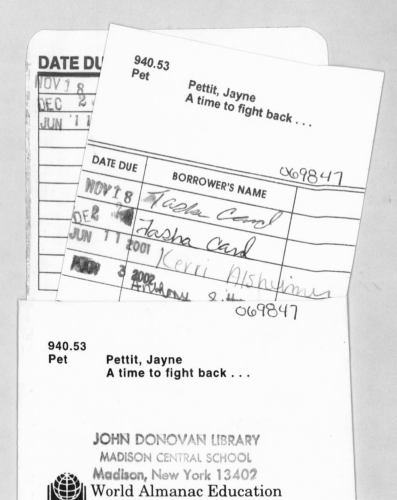